S0-EIH-751

The Gift Horse

Gill Morrell

The Gift Horse

Typeset by Roberta L. Melzl
Editor: Bobbie Chase
Printed in Germany, 2010

ISBN: 978-1-934983-48-5

Stabenfeldt, Inc.
225 Park Avenue South
New York, NY 10003
www.pony4kids.com

Available exclusively through PONY.

Chapter One

I wrapped my arms around Dandy's dappled neck and buried my face in his long mane. His pony smell was gorgeous – warm and spicy – and the coarse hairs tickled my nose.

"It'll be our turn to jump next, Dandy boy," I whispered. "But, not too fast, okay?"

In the riding school, my twin sister Ruby was just about to start her round. Smoke swished his gray tail excitedly as he pranced up to the first jump. Ruby tightened the reins and leaned forward eagerly. They soared over the low wall, jumping much higher than they needed to, and Smoke landed badly, stumbling and lurching sideways. Ruby nearly bounced right off, but she grabbed a handful of his mane with one hand and the saddlebow with the other, got herself settled well down in the saddle, and yelled, "Go on!"

He raced to the next fence, a hog's back with three bars, one after the other, the middle one higher than the other two. Smoke took off enthusiastically and cleared it easily again, and this time Ruby stayed with her pony, her head right by his neck like a proper show jumper, her dark curly hair bouncing as it escaped from her hard hat. Three jumps to go ... The next was a low post and rails which they popped over with no fuss at all. Now there was a double; first a low gate and then a cross pole, one after the other, close enough to require careful riding. Smoke was pulling, but Ruby didn't seem at all bothered. She lengthened the reins and let him have his head and he leaped over the first obstacle, took one long stride, and took off for the second. I could see instantly that they were much too far away. I sort of jumped with them, willing Smoke to stretch just that little bit further to clear the bar. Ruby was going to be so disappointed if she got a fault, she wanted a clear round so badly ... but, wow, they *were* over! Just one jump to go.

On her way, Ruby cantered past the railings where I was waiting with Dandy, and flashed me a quick, triumphant smile.

"Be careful!" I shouted automatically, but she was past me and accelerating toward the final jump. It was parallel bars over straw bales, which meant that Smoke would have to stretch again. This time she held him back so he wouldn't take off so early, with the result that they actually took off way too late. Smoke had to leap almost vertically and then somehow straighten out to stay in the air. I held my breath and closed my eyes. They were going to hit the last bar, I knew they were, and then Ruby would be devastated...

Then everyone around me was clapping and Dad shouted out, "Great stuff, Ruby!" and it was all over. A clear round. I was so proud of my twin.

I cheered with everyone else, but now there was a

sinking feeling in my stomach. My turn next. How on earth was I going to get around without falling off or making a fool of myself?

Tanya, who runs the Foxton Stables where we ride in our village, and who'd organized this competition day as a rousing start to the summer vacation, grabbed Smoke's noseband and steadied him.

"Quite a round, Ruby," she said drily. "Not exactly what I'd describe as controlled, but a brave ride. Well done."

Ruby grinned happily. Her feet dangled free of her stirrups as she guided Smoke around the outside of the ring to where I was waiting.

"Told you I'd do it," she said happily. "I bet I was the fastest, too. Faster than Hannah, even."

Hannah's our best friend. Ruby and I had always used the Foxton ponies, but Hannah was lucky enough to have her own pony, and Socks was just about the liveliest pony I'd ever seen. He was always eager to canter and never hesitated to jump. When the jumping competition was announced, Ruby challenged Hannah to a private contest, and now it looked as if she'd won. Socks had gotten around the course pretty fast, too, but he'd knocked a couple of bars down, which gave him eight faults. Hannah had had to slow him down a couple times, too, before the bigger jumps.

Dad came over, eyes glued to the stopwatch on his cell phone. "That was one minute thirty-three," he said, enthusiastically.

"What did Hannah get?" Ruby asked quickly.

"One minute forty-eight, and she had all those faults, too. No one else is anywhere near you. You'll have won easily. Good girl!"

7

"Thanks to Smoke," said Ruby, stroking him lovingly, "and there's still Poppy to go, don't forget."

Dad slapped Dandy's broad shoulder. "Not that you've got much chance on this old slug," he commented.

"Dad, don't be so mean!" I said indignantly. "That's such a horrible thing to say about Dandy. Anyway, he's not a slug. He just doesn't see why he should rush."

"No more than you do," said Dad. I went red. He patted my shoulder. "Try to prove me wrong. Go on, it's your turn now, isn't it?'"

Tanya was shouting for me, so I didn't hang around to try to convince Dad about Dandy. It would be a waste of time, anyway. Dad was mostly interested in our winning, and he was right about one thing, at least. Dandy was, as far as I was concerned, the best pony in the world, but he was no rocket. He was totally different from Smoke; much like Ruby and me, really.

Ruby and I are twins, and of course we love each other but we're definitely not clones. For a start, we don't look alike. We're what are known as fraternal twins, and so most people wouldn't even guess we're sisters. Ruby's tall and, as I mentioned, she's got wavy brown hair and a turned up nose and everyone says how mature she looks. She actually needs to wear a bra, whereas I'm still totally flat. On top of that, I'm a lot shorter. We're both pretty slim, though. My hair is shoulder length, like hers, but straight and blonde. I don't think I'm so nice looking, although Dad says I am. Well, he would, wouldn't he? There's only him; Mom died in a car accident when we were six. We all miss her still, but somehow we've gotten used to it being just the three of us.

Ruby and I used to do almost everything together. We

were in the same class in elementary school and shared a bedroom and all that, but now that we were almost twelve things had changed. We were fighting about all sorts of silly things and it seemed that now, when we disagreed about something, we didn't always instinctively understand each other the way we always used to.

When we moved up to junior high last September, we were put in different classes, too. That was really strange at first, and also, Ruby got to spend much more time with Hannah than I did, as they were in the same class, and I hadn't found anyone else that I liked as much. Anyway, nearly a year later, the one thing we all three still loved to do together was riding. Ruby and I didn't do it for the same reasons. Ruby's ambition was to ride the fastest, most challenging ponies possible and she dreamed of being a three-day eventer at the Olympic Games. I absolutely loved being among the ponies and getting to know them, but I didn't much like jumping or galloping. Even though we squabbled a lot nowadays, our different outlooks on riding hadn't been an issue between us. I was just more cautious by nature, and Ruby more daring. It wasn't a big deal.

I was getting butterflies as I walked Dandy into the riding school. The clip-clop of his hoofs was muffled by the soft surface as I walked him in a circle, putting off the moment of starting my round. To be honest, I'd have much preferred just to watch the jumping competition, but Dad, always hopeful that I'll do as well as Ruby, wouldn't have let me miss it.

"Go for it, Poppy!" yelled Ruby from behind me. I gathered the reins carefully and did what I'd planned when I was lying in bed worrying the night before; I focused on the first jump and ignored the rest.

Dandy responded to my shaking the reins and pressing my heels into his sides with a slow trot, and I guided him toward the wall. It wasn't high really. He hardly had to lift off the ground to clear it. He landed gently, and trotted on steadily. Fine, I thought, maybe we can do this after all.

Dandy pricked his ears as we approached the hog's back, still at a trot, and for a split second I imagined us soaring over it spectacularly and everyone clapping and cheering. But no, he plodded up, jumped just high enough to scrape over, and came to an immediate stop on the other side.

"Darling Dandy, please, at least *try*," I whispered, trying to kick him on gently. Luckily, he responded by trotting again. I leaned forward the way you're supposed to, looked ahead at the post and rails, and willed him to want to get over it, but he wasn't eager, and swerved away to the side. Gritting my teeth, I kept him going and steered a big circle so that we were approaching the jump again. He must have realized I needed him to jump, because he didn't hesitate this time and we got over in one piece.

"Push him on, Poppy!" That had to be Dad, of course. I wanted to impress him with how my riding had improved, so I leaned forward again and kicked harder and Dandy actually started to canter.

"Sit into the saddle and drive him on," Tanya called from the railings, where she was perched watching us. The double was right in front of me. In theory, I knew all about getting the stride right, but in reality I just pointed Dandy in the right direction and hoped. I think I shut my eyes. We bounced up and down; he did a couple of quick, jerky steps. We went up and down again and, to my amazement, we'd cleared the double. There was only one fence to go.

Maybe I'd even get a clear round, apart from that refusal. Maybe I'd even beat Hannah!

But Dandy, obviously and quite reasonably, thought he'd done enough for one afternoon. He slowed down to a trot again and when we reached the last fence, with its wide stretch, he just stopped. I toppled forward in slow motion over his lowered head and saw the straw bales looming up toward me. With my feet firmly in the stirrups and my knees stuck to Dandy's sides, somehow I stopped myself falling.

"Take him back around," Tanya called. I gathered the reins and gave him another firm kick and got him into a sort of canter. We circled once and then I pointed him at the jump and tried again. Please jump it, I willed, please don't make me look stupid; please show how clever you are. He must've read my mind. He cantered right up to the fence, took off and tried his absolute best to clear it.

He almost succeeded, too. We only knocked the second bar down, with a clatter that echoed around the ring, but I didn't care. We'd completed our round with only two refusals and one fence down and I was really happy. The moment we were out of the ring, with scattered applause echoing in our ears, I slithered off and went to Dandy's head to stroke and pet him for being so brave and clever, and to thank him for not letting me fall.

"Great stuff!" shouted Ruby, running over. "I never thought you'd get over the double. You rode that really well."

"It was all Dandy, not me," I said, balancing half a carrot on my palm so he could have a reward.

"Don't let Tanya see you give him that while he's got his bit in," warned Hannah, trotting up on Socks. "Yuck, he's dribbling everywhere."

11

"Yes, but he deserves it," I insisted, trying to hide Dandy's orange moustache from Tanya's eagle eyes. "You know how I hate jumping, and he did great."

"Take some of the credit for yourself," advised Ruby.

"And what credit is that exactly?"

It was Dad. He was looking really disappointed and my heart sank. I'd let him down.

"Didn't Poppy do a great round?" said Hannah loyally, but Dad didn't soften; in fact, he looked annoyed.

"You'll never get anywhere if you insist on riding the wrong pony," he said sharply, "and I told you at the start that this one wouldn't do anything. It could hardly get around. I'll have a word with Tanya and ask her to find you another one for the rest of the afternoon."

He started off toward her.

"Dad, please!" I cajoled. Dad can seem tough, but he really loves us so it's not completely impossible to change his mind.

He stopped in his tracks and looked back.

"What?"

"There are only a few games to go. Can't I just stay on Dandy for those? He's really good at the flag race," I added, knowing Dad would like that.

"As long as you ride to win. If I've told you once, I've told you a million times, winning is what matters. It took you two minutes and thirty seconds to do those five jumps, and he still knocked one of them down."

"It wasn't Dandy's fault ..."

Dad just looked at me, and raised an eyebrow.

"Yes, Dad," I muttered. There was no point in arguing. To him there's only one aim in life; to do better than the opposition. He's always telling us how he started out as an ordinary plumber and made good, and now runs his own company. I know he hopes we'll be as ambitious and hard working as he is.

Anyway, he joined the other parents who were bunched together on benches, chatting and passing out drinks. None of *them* seemed to be obsessed with their children winning.

The three of us exchanged rueful glances.

"Cheer up," said Hannah, giving me a hug. Her long brown braid swung around and caught me in the eye. "Sorry! Look, just remember how well you did, and think about that flag race."

The last competitor finished jumping and Tanya strode into the center of the ring and shouted for silence.

"Well done, everyone," she said. "So, results – Hannah's third with eight faults, Ellie second with three, and Ruby got our only clear round on Smoke."

Hannah and Ruby vaulted onto their ponies; both tall and slender, they cantered in to get rosettes, to more applause. I clapped as hard as I could. Part of me wished I could have been in there too, but then Dandy nuzzled my armpit from behind and made me jump. I fondled his soft nose and told myself not to be silly.

I knew Dandy would love the flag race. Plus, I was going to be at a definite advantage when it came to lifting the flags out of their holders, as Dandy was small so I could lean far over. This could be my bit of glory, my chance to shine. I was determined to end the day really well.

We all lined up at one end of the ring. I patted Dandy's firm neck encouragingly and he pricked his ears intelligently. I psyched myself up to push him straight into a canter, even though it meant kicking him hard. Next to me, Socks was pulling at his bit, eager to be off, and further along the line Smoke was, I knew, ready to win again. I glanced over to the benches where Dad was sitting next to Hannah's mom. She waved cheerfully and nudged Dad, who was fiddling with his beloved cell phone. But then he looked up, grinned at me and gave me a thumbs-up sign. I knew he'd be watching. No pressure, then.

The sudden whistle made me jump and must have startled Dandy, too, because he shot off and we reached the far end where the flags were in record time. I yanked one out of its holder and swung Dandy back around to face the start. He cantered back to the starting line so quickly that we were the first there. I threw the flag down and yanked the right rein to turn Dandy toward the next flag. He'd gotten agitated now, and fought my instructions, and by the time we were pointing in the right direction and cantering again, a couple of other ponies were ahead of us. Ruby was still on her way back to the start, trying to persuade Smoke to keep in a straight line, and as we passed her she dropped her flag and had to go back for another one.

"Come on, Dandy!" I urged, shaking the reins and willing him on, and as we reached the flags, we caught up with the ponies in front. I grabbed the flag and we turned, but in my excitement I fumbled and dropped it!

"Get another!" Dad yelled.

Dandy responded fantastically. We swerved back past the flags, and the second I got hold of one he was off, galloping toward the start, overtaking one of the leaders as we went.

On the next run, we drew parallel with Hannah, who was leading, and she threw me a grin of pure happiness as our ponies scrambled in unison around the flag holders and

14

set off for the start again. That was three flags collected – two to go.

I had no idea what the other ponies were doing by now. The contest was between Hannah and me, or rather between Dandy and Socks. We stayed perfectly even as we went up and down and up again. As I leaned forward to grab the last flag, Socks swerved past, the white bands on his chestnut legs gleaming in the sunlight. I kicked Dandy on and shouted, "Go, go, go!" Clutching the flag with whitened knuckles, I lifted myself from the saddle and leaned forward like a jockey. We seemed to fly that last time down the ring, and I couldn't even have told you where Socks and Hannah were. All I could focus on was getting back to the start without dropping that flag.

We were there! I let go of the flag and hauled on the reins to stop Dandy, who was hoping for yet another run at the course. The moment he'd halted, I slid off and pulled the reins over his head, holding them close to the bit to control him. I'd never seen him so excited, he was practically foaming at the mouth, but I'm sure he was as thrilled as I was.

Hannah skidded to a stop and let go of the reins so Socks could lower his head.

"Who won?" she said, patting him ecstatically.

"I don't know. Wasn't that just great, though?"

"Totally cool. It was one of us two, I'm sure."

The others milled around us, and we waited for the result.

"Poppy, well done," said Tanya. "I don't know what you did to Dandy, but that's the fastest I've ever seen him go. And Hannah, too, that was an excellent ride. Well, it's between the two of you, and it was almost a dead heat, but one of the ponies just stuck his nose ahead at the crucial moment."

She paused dramatically and you could have heard a pin drop.

"Poppy, congratulations," she said. "You've won by a nose. Come and get your rosette."

Chapter Two

I scrambled back onto Dandy to go and get our rosette, stroking him wildly. Hannah followed on Socks and, to my surprise, Ruby collected third place. That meant both of them had two rosettes each to my one, but I didn't care. I dismounted and led Dandy to the benches for Dad's congratulations. He'd have to admit it now – Dandy was *not* a slug.

But Dad wasn't there.

"Well done, Poppy, you must be really pleased," said Hannah's mom, giving me a hug. She understood how I felt about riding.

"Where's Dad?"

"Busy; give him a moment."

He was talking on the phone as usual, so I ran over to him and grabbed his free arm.

"Dad, wasn't that great? Dandy was so fantastic!"

"Shhh."

I was so excited that I danced from one foot back to the other until he finally disconnected. "You won? Oh, well done, Poppy, that's very good. Such a shame it was only a game and not the jumping. Never mind, things'll be different next time. Hang on a minute, now, I've got to call back."

I felt my cheeks flood red with mixed anger and disappointment. He hadn't known I'd won, I thought. He hadn't been watching, and he didn't care anyway. And why should "next time" be any different?

Ruby joined us, full of praise for Dandy and me, but she too went quiet when she saw Dad's preoccupation with his phone. It was odd – it didn't sound like a work call. He was making some kind of arrangements for Monday. It was our birthday on Monday.

"I hope Dad's not going to have to be out *all* day," I whispered to Ruby.

"Umm, he did say he'd be at home for a while, didn't he?"

"He's sure to try. He's never missed the day."

At last, Dad pressed the off button and looked up. He had a great big grin plastered over his face.

"Well, girls, I didn't want to tell you till it was completely settled, but your birthday present is finally all organized. And do you want to know what it is?"

We certainly did. Dad had been very mysterious about our presents, refusing to tell us anything in advance except that it would be a joint one, and we'd had all sorts of theories about it.

"It'll be arriving on your birthday on Monday. Perfect timing."

"Yes, but what is 'it'?" Ruby and I spoke in unison.

18

Dad rubbed his hands together in the way he does when he's made a really good deal.

"I decided it's time you had a pony, a proper show jumper, so you can take part in all the shows you want. No more riding school ponies for my two gorgeous girls – you're getting a pony of your very own!"

Ruby's face lit up. Eyes shining, she gave Dad the most enormous hug.

"Thank you a million times! That's perfect, the best birthday surprise imaginable!"

"Only what you deserve," Dad said, hugging her back. "And you too, Poppy," he added, grinning at me over Ruby's head. "Just think what you'll be able to achieve now."

I nodded, unable to speak for excitement. To think I'd been thinking mean things about Dad, when he was actually organizing such an amazing present for us.

"Tell us about the pony," demanded Ruby.

"Well, he's named Thunder, and from everything I've heard, he'll live up to his name. He's got a good record of winning, especially jumping, and his old owners say he's bold and brave and just right for good riders."

My heart sank a little. That didn't actually sound like my sort of pony. The ones I like are gentle and easygoing.

"When do we get to see him?" asked Ruby eagerly.

"First thing on Monday, as I said. The horse trailer is arriving at nine. Lucky it's vacation, eh? I'll go into work late so I can meet him too."

"Haven't you seen him, then?" I asked in surprise. How could you choose something as important as a pony, that'd be a central part of our lives, without checking him out first?

Dad stretched out his spare arm and put it around my shoulders so we were cuddled up against him, one on each side, the way we all liked.

"I've bought him off an Internet site," he explained. "At the moment he's ridden by a girl who's grown too tall for him. So I just paid an agent to look at him for us. After all, I'm not exactly a pony expert, am I? Not like you two, my two champion riders."

I felt a glow of pride that Dad was recognizing my achievement in the flag race. He must be feeling really pleased to include me with Ruby's win, I thought. Maybe in the future, I'd be able to do just as well. I thought back to how it had felt a few minutes earlier, whizzing toward the finishing line, at one with my pony. Perhaps from now on I'd enjoy that sort of riding more, on our own pony!

"What's he look like?" Ruby and I asked at the same moment. We giggled at each other excitedly.

"Here, I've got a picture of him on my phone, but there's a better one on the computer at home." Dad showed us the screen. The pony that stood sideways in the picture looked very grand, maybe a little too grand for my taste. He had a neatly braided mane and tail, with none of that gorgeous shagginess that ponies should have. He was very shiny, glossy black, and you could just glimpse a white blaze down his nose. Ruby grabbed my hand to squeeze it.

"He looks perfect, Dad, absolutely perfect, and you couldn't have chosen a better present, could he, Poppy?"

I swallowed hard. Don't be ridiculous, I thought. You can't not want a pony because it's too good. I smiled at Dad and agreed with Ruby.

Tanya joined us. "Have you broken the news to the twins? You're a lucky pair, getting a pony with such a good track record in shows. I'm looking forward to settling him in here."

"We *are* keeping him here, then?"

"Where else?" said Dad. "I want Tanya to keep on teaching you, anyhow, and we've hardly got enough space in the back yard at home for a pony! But you two will have to do all the hard work of looking after him, okay? I'm renting stable space; "livery" they call it, but not Tanya's labor."

That was what Hannah did already with Socks, so we weren't surprised. I adored looking after ponies and always helped Hannah when I could. I loved it, too, when Tanya asked us to help with grooming and feeding and mucking out the riding school ponies, whereas Ruby got bored when she was told to do all that. I could see myself spending a lot of time at the stables. There'd always be a reason to be there from now on. Thunder ... Maybe, despite his alarming name and all this stuff about him being so bold, he'd be as sweet and easy to ride as Dandy.

The minute we got home we rushed to look at the details on the website. It said Thunder was thirteen hands, which would be about the same as Smoke but quite a lot bigger than Dandy. Even I had to admit that I was getting a little tall for Dandy. It showed Thunder standing sideways and also jumping cross-poles, looking very impressive. The blurb said he was a great pony for teenagers ready for a challenge, which worried me. First of all, we weren't going to be teenagers for another year, and, second, I wasn't looking for too many challenges. But Ruby was so ecstatic, and Hannah and all our friends were so excited as well, that I got swept away by the whole thing.

Ruby and I talked ponies nonstop for the rest of the weekend and didn't quarrel once. We were both awake at five on Monday morning, watching the sun rise and planning how we'd spend the rest of the day. At six, we went down for breakfast and then hung around until Dad came down. Then we got our cards and opened presents from our grandmother and some other relatives. Most people still gave us joint presents, something bigger that might not be what one of us actually wanted, but Gran had always insisted on treating us as individuals.

This year she'd bought Ruby a DVD about three-day eventing, and for me she got a book of stories about ponies. Gran knew that I was the one who always wanted to read rather than watch TV.

Just before nine Hannah arrived, bringing us cool presents from her and her family. She gave us a manual on stable management, "Because you'll need that with your own pony," and her mother had bought us T-shirts like the ones Hannah was wearing that summer, much skimpier and more fitted than our old ones.

Mine was deep blue – Hannah said her mom had tried to match my eyes – and Ruby's was yellow.

"Not to match mine, I hope," she said. Her eyes were a sort of brownish-green color.

"Course not," laughed Hannah.

"The color suits you, though, it looks right against your hair," I added.

We put the T-shirts on and admired each other and then all three of us sat on the garden wall, swinging our legs over the pavement, watching for the horse trailer to come into view. It was so exciting.

At last there was a rumbling noise and around the corner

came a Land Rover towing an elegant horse trailer. Dad came out as it stopped and we jumped to the ground and ran around to the back to get our first glimpse of Thunder, but the doors were firmly shut. We joined the grownups, who were shaking hands and talking about the journey and all that boring adult stuff, when what they should've been doing was opening the trailer so we could meet our pony. Our pony! We had to say hello to the driver, who went on and on about how it was his daughter who'd owned and ridden Thunder for the last five years. I couldn't help wondering why she hadn't bothered to come along to say goodbye and see what we were like. I couldn't imagine letting a pony of mine go to a strange home without checking it out first. Then, at long last, everyone went over to the doors and we finally got to see *our* pony.

He was tied up with his back to us so the first thing we saw was his backside. Three things struck me right away. He was very, very black. There didn't seem to be a spot of white anywhere. He was miles taller than any pony I'd ever ridden. And in contrast to Dandy, who could be kindly described as solidly built and less kindly as a little fat, he was pretty skinny, even bony.

He was backed out of the horse trailer with a good amount of trouble. There wasn't room for him to turn and he refused at first to go backwards. His old owner had to tug at his head collar for a long time to get him moving. Then, when he'd clattered down the ramp and was standing in the road, we finally got to see him properly.

The white blaze was really dramatic, but his face was as narrow as the rest of him, with none of that cuddliness which most ponies have. It was like he was looking down his nose at us in a really suspicious manner, as if we were way below him. And his coal black coat wasn't particularly shiny in real life.

Ruby and Hannah clearly felt totally differently about him. They were both full of admiration.

"Look at his mane, it's so beautiful!" breathed Hannah. I looked; it had been braided really tightly, like in the photo we'd seen. I tried to smile, but inside I wished it had been let free. Still, I thought, he's our pony now, and the first thing I'm going to do is to undo all those fiddly knots and allow him to feel the wind in his mane the way ponies should. His tail looked just like a sausage in its tight braid; I couldn't imagine why anyone would think that was nicer that having it loose. Still, as Hannah almost always wore her hair in a long braid, I suppose that's what looked good to her.

"Happy, twins?" asked Dad, with a broad smile.

Ruby was jumping with excitement, and it wasn't hard for me to pretend to look pleased and let her have all the attention. No way did I want to hurt Dad's feelings when he'd been so generous.

Dad told us to lead Thunder along the road to the stables; it's only a ten-minute walk, to the far end of our village. He shook hands with the old owner and that was that. The Land Rover and horse trailer rattled past us a few moments later. A disembodied hand waved, and Thunder was all ours.

He didn't much like the Land Rover going by. He skittered sideways with a clatter of hoofs, tossing his head and rolling his eyes dramatically. Ruby and Hannah had to hang on tight to stop him from backing into the center of the road. Ours is a fairly quiet village, but there's always an occasional passing car. I prayed this was just first day nerves and that Thunder wasn't going to be a problem in traffic. Surely that would be something Dad and his expert would have checked out? It certainly didn't seem so; every time a car came by there was the same tug of war. I stayed at the back, well clear of Thunder's hoofs, worried.

When we got to the stables, there was no one around. Foxton Stables is pretty small, with just a dozen ponies and a few more that belong to local children. Tanya ran it alone. That was good from my point of view, because she liked us to help out sometimes when she was busy. Tanya was young enough to be fun, too, though she could be strict and a little sarcastic when she felt like it.

Ruby and Hannah tied Thunder's head collar rope to a ring on the wall and stood back. I was expecting them to be a little concerned after the last ten minutes, but they were anything but. They both seemed enchanted.

"What do you think?" I said tentatively. "He might be a little big ..."

"No, he's not, and he's so slim and elegant," countered Ruby. She looked at me. "Oh no. You're not going to *not* like him, are you, Poppy? He's absolutely gorgeous." She sounded incredulous that anyone couldn't fall in love with him instantly.

"I only meant he's a lot taller than I'm used to," I said weakly. "He must be over fourteen hands."

"Dad said thirteen."

"Isn't that the whole point, anyway, a pony you can ride for years and years?" Hannah enthused. "Don't get stressed, Poppy. It's just that he's thin, and it makes him look taller."

"Yes, like that man said, his daughter had him for years.

Just think, he'll be ours till we're about sixteen! And he's so, so beautiful."

There was a clatter of hooves and we turned around to see Tanya on her gray horse, Roland. She jumped down quickly, tied Roland to his stable door, and hurried over to meet Thunder.

"Isn't he beautiful!" she said at once. "Okay, let's have a good look at him."

She started at Thunder's head, patting his neck and looking at his eyes and then pulling down his lips to look at his teeth. "He's about nine years old, girls, can you see? Those little hooks on his teeth, do you see, they develop around then and later they wear away again. How long was he with his last owner?"

"Five years," I said.

"Well, he's still young, in the prime of life. You should get years of good use from him. Now let's see..."

Tanya moved to Thunder's side, patted him and slid her hand down the pony's front leg, lifting his hoof. Thunder was completely calm and obedient now that she was in charge and I felt reassured. Maybe he'd just acted up with Hannah and Ruby because we were young.

"He's in pretty good condition," Tanya concluded a few minutes later, "though he could use a good grooming. He looks like he's got a lot of energy and oomph. Just right for you, Ruby."

Ruby nodded eagerly.

Tanya looked at me.

"And what do you think of him, Poppy?" she asked kindly.

"I'm really looking forward to grooming him and all that," I said carefully. "But maybe I shouldn't actually ride him till I grow slightly bigger."

26

"Oh, we'll make sure you learn to ride him. I'm sure he's been very well schooled. And he's not really too big for you; your dad said a shade over thirteen hands, didn't he?" She paused and looked at me properly. "Let's check. Ruby and Hannah, run and get the measuring stick from the top shelf in the tack room."

As soon as they were gone, she put her arm around my shoulders and spoke quietly. "Don't you worry, Poppy, he'll be a great ride, you'll see."

"I still like Dandy better," I whispered back.

"Cheer up! It *is* your birthday and you *have* been given your own pony. That's not exactly a disaster, is it?" She paused for a moment. "The only thing is, Poppy, your dad's paid a lot for Thunder and understandably he doesn't want to waste his money, so you'll be taking lessons just on your own pony from now on."

"But ..."

Tanya hurried on. "There's nothing to stop you taking turns, and having your own pony's a very expensive business. After all, why should your dad pay for extra lessons on my ponies?"

It had never occurred to me that getting Thunder might mean never riding Dandy. Ruby and I had imagined that we'd take turns on our own pony and then use the riding school ponies for the rest of the time, and I'd privately decided that my turn for Thunder wouldn't happen very often. But if we were only allowed to ride him exclusively, there would be two alternatives. Either I'd have to ride Thunder and get over my fears, or I'd never ride at all.

On top of that, how did Dad think we were going to manage during the group lessons? Half an hour each? One of us doing all the preliminary schooling and the other one the jumping and stuff? And what about trail riding?

My gloomy thoughts were interrupted when the other two ran back, waving the long wooden stick marked off in four-inch sections. Tanya held it so one end was on the ground and read off the measurement where it reached the top of Thunder's withers.

"He is actually a little over thirteen two, but that's good really as he'll be useful to you for years to come, though you'll have to stay slim, both of you; he's certainly no heavyweight. So, who's going to have the first ride?"

"Dad's bringing the tack down in the car in a few minutes," I stalled. "Should we show him his stable?"

"Why don't we turn him out into the paddock with all the others so they can make friends?" suggested Ruby.

"He's got to meet Socks!" added Hannah. "Maybe they'll be best friends, like us?"

"I think we'll keep him on his own for a while, till we get to know him. We'll let him get to know the other ponies gradually," said Tanya. "He'll be in the end stall, next to the big box, but you may as well leave him here for the moment. You've got a lesson booked for ten, and he'll be fine. I'll fix up Roland and see you in a minute."

"Can Hannah have her lesson then too?"

"Not this time. Your dad's booked you an individual session so you can get to know Thunder. Why don't you watch, Hannah?"

"Try getting rid of me!" Hannah joked. "I can't wait to see him in action."

We stood around looking at our new pony. He was getting restless, tossing his head again and stamping his off-hind hoof, as if he was bored. Ruby fed him some pony nuts and stroked his neck, but I didn't want to get near; his eyes looked a little wild to me and I wasn't eager to get stepped on. At long last, Dad drove in and I ran over to get the tack, glad for an excuse to get away from Thunder. Dad helped me by carrying the saddle, which was good quality but not very shiny. Maybe Thunder's old owner hadn't enjoyed keeping it clean as I would. I let Ruby put on the bridle; I wasn't too sure about putting my fingers near the pony's mouth in case he decided to bite me. Then I hefted the saddle onto his back. It was a big reach for me. I didn't duck under his stomach to cross to the other side, the way I'd normally do. I went around the back, leaving a wide berth, just in case. I fastened the girth and pulled down the stirrups. It was time for one of us to mount.

Chapter Three

"You go first," I said quickly. "I won't mind waiting."

"You sure?" Ruby had her foot in the nearside stirrup and was mounted within seconds. She sorted the reins into her left hand and swung her right leg forward to check the girth. I hadn't wanted to pull it too tight, so Ruby took the buckle in another two notches. Then she adjusted the stirrup leathers and settled herself comfortably.

"How does he feel?" asked Dad, holding the bridle in a proprietary way and leading Thunder toward the gateway into the enclosed riding school where we had our lessons.

"Great! He's way thinner than Smoke, and his neck's narrow too. Strange, but he's really cool. Please let go, Dad, I can manage."

Dad stood back and we all watched as Ruby walked Thunder around the perimeter of the school. He was obviously longing to stretch his legs; he fidgeted and extended his neck, and even bucked a little bit.

Tanya got Ruby to walk him around and around for a while, until he calmed right down. They looked great together.

"You can trot on," called Tanya eventually, "whenever you're ready."

"Great. Okay, everyone, watch this."

Thunder was so eager to get going, Ruby barely had to give any aids. Tanya got her to go through lots of changes, from walk to trot and to canter and back again. By the end of half an hour, they were cantering fast around the ring, doing figure eights.

"Can I jump him now?" Ruby called.

Tanya shook her head.

"Not today. Get used to his pace and wait till he's settled in," she said. "He's pretty lively. I don't want you to lose control."

"Oh, go on, let her have a try," Dad said.

"I don't think it's wise, not this first time," Tanya said firmly. "Anyway, it must be Poppy's turn."

Dad frowned and Tanya looked back steadily. Hannah and I exchanged glances. There was nothing new about this. Dad was always suggesting bigger and better riding challenges and Tanya was very clever at getting out of them if she didn't approve.

"Bring him to a controlled halt, Ruby," she called.

"It can't really be Poppy's turn yet, can it?" she shouted back, keeping Thunder at a steady canter.

"Yes, it is!"

"Fair shares, Ruby," Dad called at the same time as Tanya. That always worked on both of us. We'd always shared so much, and neither of us liked the other one to lose out. Ruby slowed Thunder and brought him through

31

the gateway to halt neatly where we were waiting. She slid off and handed me the reins.

"Okay?" I said, nervously.

"Just fantastic! Look after him now."

A bunch of other riders had assembled, ready for their lesson after us, and lined up along the rails, watching us. That made me nervous. It seemed like a long reach up to Thunder's withers, and there was no comfortable chunk of flowing mane to grab hold of. It was a real stretch to get my left foot in the stirrup; in fact I only just got the tip of my toe in, but I decided to get on with things. I pushed off from my right foot as best I could, snatched at the back of the saddle with my right hand, and was halfway up when Thunder sidestepped away from me. Because I hadn't had enough spring and hadn't really gotten hold of anything properly, there wasn't anything I could do. I fell backwards, letting go of the reins, and landed with a thump on my backside. I looked like a total idiot.

I could just feel everyone looking at me in a pitying kind of way, and worse, I could hear stifled giggles. I scrambled to my feet and looked around wildly. Hannah and Ruby were holding their mouths closed. I stuck my tongue out at them crossly.

"Sorry, Poppy, but it looked so funny," Hannah managed to say before the giggles started again.

"Lucky there wasn't a puddle," added Ruby, fighting back her laughter.

"Or a pile of poop!"

"That's quite enough, girls," said Tanya, severely. They calmed down immediately. She'd got the bridle right by the bit and was holding Thunder steady. "Have another try, Poppy."

"Sorry, I should've hung onto him."

Ruby gave my arm an affectionate squeeze. "I didn't think, I was so pleased with him."

I can never stay cross with Ruby when she apologizes. I returned the squeeze, took a deep breath, and turned to face Thunder again. He stared at me scornfully, down his long nose.

This time, I stretched my foot into the stirrup properly and settled into the saddle. It felt really strange after Dandy. My legs were so much closer together than usual, and his neck looked like the sharp angle at the front of a boat. The knobby parts of mane stuck up uncomfortably, making me feel sorry for him, even though I knew perfectly well that it didn't hurt him to have it like that. I leaned forward and gave him a tentative pat, and felt his skin quiver nervously under my hand.

Tanya helped me adjust the stirrup leathers and made sure the girth was still tight, and then led us into the ring.

"Walk him steadily," she said quietly, "you can do it."

I pressed my heels against Thunder's sides and he moved off so quickly that I wobbled around and had to grab the saddlebow. I hung on tightly as Thunder took me around the ring, not trying to do anything more than stay on him.

Tanya met me three quarters of the way around, where we were out of earshot of most of the spectators.

"Okay, Poppy, so far so good, now let go of the saddle and start riding."

She sounded impatient, and I felt a little hurt.

"Come on, try! He looks like a great ride."

Ruby and Hannah had sprinted around to join us and were watching eagerly.

33

"You don't need to be frightened of him," Ruby added, "he won't bite."

I knew I was being ridiculously wimpy. I sat up straight, took the reins properly into both hands, and settled my feet firmly into the stirrups.

Once I was riding Thunder, and not just being carried along, it was a lot better. I went around and around at a walk, sometimes changing direction – and he *did* respond when I asked him to turn. Dad was looking pleased, and on the third circuit I felt safe enough to push Thunder into a trot and that was also okay. In fact, I was starting to relax and enjoy myself.

Thunder seemed to sense the exact moment that I wasn't fully concentrating. He tossed his head and the reins pulled through my fingers, stinging them. With close contact gone, he broke into a canter.

"Control him, Poppy!" called Tanya, and I hauled the reins toward me, but every time they got shorter, Thunder tossed his head again and I lost them. We were going fast now, and all I could think about was trying not to fall off.

I suppose it could have been a lot worse. Tanya used her voice to order him to stop. He was obviously used to obeying as he halted and stood still, looking at her as if for instructions. So far as Thunder was concerned, I might just as well have been a sack of potatoes tied to his back.

"Can I stop now?" I panted.

"In a while. Let's just get you riding him again," she said. 'We can't have you losing your nerve."

Dad came into the ring. He stroked Thunder's neck and didn't seem to notice how jumpy he was, or that I'd been having a hard time. To be honest, he doesn't know much about riding.

"That was good stuff, Poppy," he said approvingly. "It's nice to see you letting yourself go a while on a pony that's got a little fire in him. Well, I'll be off to work now. See you later, girls."

As he was leaving, Tanya got me to walk Thunder around again, but I wasn't enjoying it, and Thunder just slinked along with his head down as if he was bored stiff. Dad's car zoomed off, which made Thunder spook a little, just as he had in the lane. I rode over to where the others were waiting.

"You can have the last five minutes if you like," I said to Ruby. "As an extra birthday present from me to you."

Ruby glowed with happiness and didn't seem to wonder why I was being so generous. I dismounted gratefully and ran over to the stables, pretending I needed the bathroom, but really just trying to get away. I just knew that, as far as I was concerned, Thunder was going to be a disaster.

At the end of the hour, I got involved with helping get Dandy ready and managed to avoid being part of the Thunder Appreciation Society. When the group lesson started, I stayed by the fence, watching them, and especially watching Dandy and, I have to admit, wiping away a few tears.

"Poppy, what's up?" Hannah and Ruby materialized on either side of me.

"We've untacked him and he's in his box," said Hannah.

"But we haven't rubbed him down properly yet, because I knew you'd want to help," added Ruby.

"No, that's okay, you go ahead," I said.

"Poppy, look at me," my sister ordered. I turned and faced her. There was no way I'd be able to hide my feelings from her. "What's wrong? Don't you like him?"

She sounded incredulous, and I could understand that. After all, we'd dreamed for years of having our own ponies, and we'd talked all weekend about how much fun it was going to be.

"Of course I do," I lied, "but did you know, Dad's said we can't ride any other ponies in the future."

"So, no more Dandy? But, Poppy, let's be honest, he's miles too small for you. Your feet almost touch the ground when you're on him. I know you love him, but Dad's got a point. He *is* a little sluggish, isn't he?"

I shrugged. The trouble was, I knew they were right. I *had* outgrown Dandy.

"Is that all?" asked Hannah gently.

"Well, there are the lessons." I explained what Tanya had said. The other two listened but they didn't take it very seriously.

"We'll just have to work out a schedule," said Ruby airily. "You do one lesson, I'll do the next. What you've forgotten is that we don't just ride when it's our lessons now, we ride every single day."

She looked so happy at the thought of this that I knew I'd said enough. How could I spoil her – our – birthday being a grump?

"Tanya says we have to leave Thunder to settle in for the rest of the day," Hannah said. "So why don't you two finish getting him groomed while I exercise Socks, and then tomorrow we can go for a ride together?"

She disappeared and we went over to the stable block. Thunder had poked his head over the door and was watching us warily.

"Isn't he gorgeous?" Ruby said lovingly. I realized that she really hadn't understood how I was feeling. She thought she'd gotten to the root of the problem, but in reality hadn't got anywhere near it. A wave of loneliness swept over me.

"Come on, let's rub him down. Do you want to undo his mane and tail? I know you don't like them done up like this."

I swallowed and managed a happy face. "Why don't you do his tail and I'll do the mane?" That would keep me away from his back feet, just in case.

"Let's have a race, who can undo it first."

Thunder stepped back, on edge, as we went in. Ruby wasn't bothered, of course. She just patted his flank cheerfully as she went by. I sidled in nervously and held out my hand. He sniffed it curiously and I ran my fingers over his soft muzzle and felt better.

I carefully unknotted and brushed out his mane while Ruby unraveled the tight elastic bands and stitching that secured Thunder's tail. He stamped impatiently once or twice, but when we'd finished he shook himself as if he enjoyed the sensation of his mane and tail flowing naturally.

"Aren't we lucky?" Ruby breathed, standing back and looking at our pony.

I shrugged. "Sure," I replied. I was *so* confused.

Over the next few days, we got into a new routine. First thing in the morning, since it was vacation, we'd be dropped off at Hannah's. I think we both really appreciated Hannah that year; she acted as a peacemaker whenever Ruby and I bickered. She was much calmer than either of us, and never seemed to lose her cool.

I liked her mother a lot, too, which was good as we spent a lot of time over at her house when Dad was at work. I think, no, I know, that she was really fond of us, especially as we didn't have a mother of our own to talk things through with.

Then, as soon as she let us, we'd go down to the stables.

Our first job was to groom our ponies. I gradually relaxed when I was around Thunder and started to enjoy brushing him. Even though he was so thin, he was very muscular. I was puzzled at first why his coat didn't gleam the way it had in the photos.

"They probably dampened it for the ads," Hannah suggested, "or even oiled it, like you do with hooves. To make him look good."

"I'm not sure his old owner liked him much," I ventured, not sure how Ruby would take that sort of critical comment.

"Don't be stupid," she insisted hotly. "No one couldn't love Thunder."

I didn't say anything more, but privately I was sure that Thunder had been looked after through duty more than affection. Now that they were properly brushed out, his mane and tail looked much nicer, though they were a little skimpy compared to Dandy's. By the time I'd finished with him, about a week or so, his coat was shiny and positively mirror-like, like patent leather, although his skin still shivered under my fingers when I first touched him, as if he didn't really like me yet.

For the first week, until Tanya let us leave him out all night, we'd lead Thunder out to the paddock. He would pull at the rope and break away into a canter the moment he got into the field, rushing over to say hello to the other ponies. They'd lift their heads from the grass and join him in an exhilarating romp at top speed, all tossing heads and flowing legs, which was really exciting and beautiful to watch. That part was great.

38

The next job was mucking out the stable, or helping clear droppings from the paddock. That sounds gross but it really isn't. It's especially nice in the paddock, where you can wander among the ponies, chatting to them and stroking them. When Tanya was busy teaching classes, she let us catch ponies for the next group and get them tacked up, and I often got to groom Dandy. I spent a lot of time working on Thunder's tack, too, polishing it until it glowed as much as he did.

I wasn't exactly frightened of Thunder when I wasn't riding him, because, don't get me wrong, he wasn't vicious or anything like that. On the other hand, he was jumpy, and you had to be careful to make sure he didn't put his hoof down on your foot when you were leading him, especially if a car went by, and he never looked at me in that totally trusting gooey way that ponies can do, or thrust his nose into my stomach for a cuddle.

Still, he was a pony, and he was ours, and I was getting used to him.

But riding him was different.

Chapter Four

We were allowed to ride Thunder and Socks in the paddock as long as most of the other ponies were being used, or we could exercise them in the ring, if it was empty. Tanya also let us ride down a trail that went for a mile or two toward the plains, as long as we didn't go alone. And twice a week we had a lesson with Hannah and three other people.

"I've worked out a schedule," I announced, before our first regular lesson. "I'll do the first half hour of each lesson, and you take over afterwards."

"That's fair," said Hannah, "except, shouldn't you swap who goes first? The boring part's always at the beginning."

"That's the part I like best, though," I said. I'd thought this all out in advance. "I'm actually getting interested in schooling – controlled walk and stuff like that. Dressage."

I waited for Ruby to object. She knew perfectly well that I wasn't especially into dressage. She raised her eyebrows quizzically and I thought she murmured something, but I couldn't be certain.

"Are you really sure?" Hannah persisted. "Every lesson?"

I nodded.

"If that's what you want," Ruby said casually. "It's your turn, then."

I still had to jump like mad to get onto him; I didn't like using the mounting block because Hannah and Ruby always giggled when I did and said I looked like an old lady. Was it my fault I wasn't as athletic as they were? Hannah was *so* lithe and skinny and had won prizes for gymnastics, and Ruby had longer legs than I did. It wasn't fair.

I did the slow, careful riding that warmed Thunder up: walking, trotting, and sometimes exercises like riding slow figure eights. I didn't trust Thunder not to take control, and the more nervous I got the more he sensed it, I suppose, and the more he did take control. It was what they call a vicious circle.

Then I'd dismount and hand him over to Ruby for all the cantering and jumping.

As you can imagine, Ruby was very happy about that. I think she really was a little bothered that I wasn't enjoying riding, but she sort of pushed it into the back of her mind. At home, Ruby and I didn't talk much about ponies or anything else; I buried myself in books as much as I could and steered clear of the passionate conversations she and Dad kept having about entering and winning big competitions.

I was worried that Tanya would tell Dad I wasn't making any progress, but she was very busy, and what she

41

didn't realize, because I made sure she didn't see, was that I was hardly riding at all apart from those two half hours a week.

"How are the two of you getting on?" Dad asked one evening. "Sharing Thunder okay?"

"Yes, it's fine," I said quickly.

"Great," enthused Ruby. "Today we were doing some cross country jumping..." and she launched into a detailed description, and Dad didn't seem to notice that I didn't feature in the ride.

I wouldn't like anyone to think Ruby was being mean deliberately, but she was so wrapped up in Thunder that every time I stood aside and suggested she ride instead of me, she'd grab the chance. Of course, I didn't think that was mean at all. I was grateful. Still, it wasn't that we'd talked it through and she was covering for me, which might have happened in the past. It was as if I didn't really count any more.

Hannah offered to lend me Socks a couple of times, but I always said no. Socks was fast and lively; we always said that when he was whizzing along, the four white socks that gave him his name merged into a blur. I suppose I was losing my nerve for riding; the more I didn't do it, the more I convinced myself I couldn't. I just rode Thunder as sedately as he'd let me as little as I could, and spent a lot of time keeping out of everyone's way.

Things came to a head a couple of weeks later. Tanya was organizing a Saturday morning group ride and said we could come along. Then she looked at Ruby and me and said very directly, "Poppy's turn today, I think. Ruby, can you keep yourself busy in the tack room?"

"Oh, but ..." I started, but Tanya ignored me.

"Okay," said Ruby, looking quite aggrieved. She slouched off to the tack room. Hannah grabbed my arm.

"This'll be fun," she said. "We've missed you being along with us. It's a pity Ruby can't come too, but then we all ride so much now."

It was good that Hannah was pleased. I'd gotten used to the idea that she and Ruby were a pair and that I was a little on the outside.

"Get a move on, Poppy," called Tanya.

For speed, I didn't use the mounting block; I just sprang as high as I could and, to my surprise, I landed squarely in the saddle. Feeling pleased with myself, I gathered the reins carefully and patted Thunder's neck. He spoiled things by dropping his head; I just knew he was wishing it were Ruby riding on his back and not me. A few butterflies fluttered in my stomach, but there was no time to get panicky. Tanya checked that we were all ready and led the long line down the trail.

Hannah was just behind me. As soon as the trail widened a little, she came up next to us and we started talking. It was just like old times, and the riding was fine, a gentle walk. Even I could do that without worrying.

After a while, Tanya rode back along the line to make sure everyone was all right. She didn't say anything to us, but looked approving, and then went to the front again and called for us to trot. In the ring, you have to try to make the pony trot the moment you want and not a second before or after, but out on a trail ride it's so much more relaxed. All the ponies broke into trot more or less together and Thunder just went along with the crowd.

"He's got the nicest action, really smooth," commented Hannah, jogging along next to me.

43

I realized she was right. Thunder trotted very rhythmically, and posting up and down was simple on him. I tried doing a sitting trot, and even that was easy because I was barely bumping at all. He wasn't pulling or anything, either. On the other hand, he seemed quite lethargic, as if he felt a little unenthusiastic about my riding him, or was I imagining it?

We finally got to the river bridge where we have to turn back when we trail ride out alone. In a group, we can go miles further. The ponies don't like crossing the river. It's deep, fast and makes a lot of noise, and the bridge is made of rattling wooden planks with gaps that you can see through to the water below.

Tanya led us across at a steady walk, turning in the saddle to check everyone. I held back so that I'd be last, hoping Thunder would follow the others and not make a fuss. My heart raced as he stepped forward and put a foot onto the bridge.

He stopped dead, nearly tipping me forward over his head. I could feel the tension running through his body and felt myself trembling uncontrollably. There was the most awful silence above the roar of the water.

"Ride him on," called Tanya encouragingly. "He's done this bridge several times. Don't let him act up."

I nodded and tried to get my shaking fingers to grip the reins tightly. I squeezed my legs and pressed my heels against Thunder's sides but he wasn't going anywhere.

"Give him a good kick!" called Tanya.

I half looked up and saw her and the others bunched together watching me.

"Go!" I hissed and kicked hard. Thunder lowered his head but he did take a tentative step forward, so I kicked again. We were making progress. Then, right in the middle, he stumbled scarily as one foot got caught up in a hole in the bridge, skewing me to one side.

If I came off, it was possible I could slide under the rickety rails into the water. I clung on desperately. There was a horrible moment when I could have gone either way, but somehow I tugged myself back into the saddle and thrust my feet solidly into the stirrups. I felt sick.

I kicked again, hoping to get him moving, but instead he shook his head violently. Thunder pulled at the reins, and sidestepped, taking me even closer to the edge, rolling his eyes so you could see the whites.

I just knew I'd never get him across.

"Ride him on!" Tanya called from the other side. "He's a little frightened, so you have to reassure him that he's safe."

"I can't..." I whispered between gritted teeth.

There was a clatter of hoofs as Tanya rode back onto the bridge and turned Roland carefully.

"Pull yourself together, Poppy," she said, in a firm but not unkind voice. "You've got to show him you're in charge. Use your body to encourage him."

I didn't quite know what she meant, but I was less panicky knowing she was there. I leaned forward, pressed my heels into Thunder's sides, shook the reins and clicked my tongue, and something from that effort worked. Thunder pricked his ears, placed his foot forward delicately and, this time, kept going and walked across without any fuss at all.

"See, you can do it perfectly well," said Hannah a few minutes later. We were following the others, keeping at the back, because I didn't want to see them looking at me and thinking what a bad rider I was.

"I can't. That was just horrific." I shuddered at the memory.

"No it wasn't. Thunder just got a little nervous. Don't overdramatize everything."

"I don't mean to, I just feel so tense."

"Try to think positively. Don't give up." She sounded so encouraging that I felt I had to try harder.

I swallowed. "Well, he did pay attention to me, in the end, didn't he?"

"Of course he did."

"And I got across the bridge. Tanya didn't actually have to lead us."

"Exactly. Happier?"

"Happier."

And I was for a while that afternoon, as we rode along woodland trails and up and over open hills. The sun was shining, Thunder was walking along comfortably, and I started to believe that I'd gotten past my mental block and would be able to ride him properly from now on. Hannah was just like she'd always been, cheerful and friendly. Riding behind her, I watched her long braid bounce against her slim back and noticed how exactly it matched the color of Socks's tail.

"You and Socks are the real twins, not Ruby and I," I called, and she swiveled in the saddle and grinned and made a quip about being a centaur. It was almost like normal again, except that Ruby wasn't there to join in the fun.

Then I remembered that to get home we'd need to cross a busy main road, and my confidence plummeted. I'd done it dozens of times on Dandy and knew that we'd have to gather on one side, wait until the signal was given, and then ride across firmly and positively. How on earth would I be able to do that on Thunder?

As we approached, the sound of the rush hour traffic

echoed in my ears, and it obviously got to Thunder, too.
He began to fidget and toss his head again. I could feel his
tension transmitting through the reins, and he was probably
getting the same messages back from me. Hannah could see
there was a problem brewing and rode ahead to tell Tanya,
who came back and told me to hold him steady.

"He's just a little twitchy; nothing to worry about," she
said. "We've been out on these lanes quite a lot in the last
week or two, and he's been absolutely fine with Ruby. This
is the first time you've gone trail riding, isn't it?"

I nodded. "He doesn't like traffic," I said, my heart in
my mouth. "That first day when we led him down to the
stables, he was all over the place."

"He was a little spooked, that's all," Hannah interjected.
"Nothing we couldn't handle."

"Well, you stay right by Poppy," Tanya advised, "and
both come up gently to the road with the rest of us. We'll
get you across safely, don't worry."

She went back to the front to control the crossing.

"You're sort of green," said Hannah, staring at me. "Are
you okay?"

"I think I'm going to throw up."

"That's stupid; you're only crossing a road. He's
perfectly all right. Ruby's done it lots of times."

"But that's Ruby," I started to say, but it was too late. We
were up with the other ponies, all bunched up on the grass
verge, waiting for Tanya to find a gap in the heavy traffic.
Thunder joggled and pulled until he was right at the front.
I kept the reins as tight as I possibly could. He skittered
sideways as a massive truck thundered past, and knocked
against another rider, and there was a sort of domino effect
as the whole group scattered. There was a piercing scream

47

as the girl riding Smoke was forced out into the traffic and only just avoided being hit by a car, and at the same time someone else was nearly unseated.

Tanya was understandably furious with me.

"Poppy, what's the matter with you? Keep in control; you know perfectly well how to."

"Sorry," I muttered, red-faced with shame.

"Take him to the rear," ordered Tanya, "and I'll help you once the traffic's stopped. Hannah, you go first, once I give the okay."

Tanya saw her moment and rode into the roadway, her hand raised to stop ongoing vehicles. The rest of the ride followed, neatly and without a fuss. I gripped the reins tight to keep Thunder from moving.

"Now!" called Tanya from the middle of the road, waving me on. But somehow, I just couldn't bring myself to give Thunder the signal to go. I was sure that if I did, he would bolt into the traffic, throw me, or kill himself; something disastrous. I think I actually closed my eyes in terror.

"Poppy, what on earth's the matter? You can do this, you know you can." Once again, Tanya had had to come back for me.

I shook my head, unable to speak.

"Let me hold him, and then and I'll lead you."

I let go of the reins reluctantly and Tanya passed them over Thunder's head and arranged Roland right beside us.

"Hold onto the saddle and let me take over."

The road was empty and she led Thunder across easily. He hardly reacted at all, not even when a truck came toward us and braked noisily. It was just me that was the problem, not Thunder.

All the others were watching. There were some giggles and sidelong glances and I just knew they all thought I was a total loser. If Thunder had really behaved badly, at least my fears would have been justified. As it was, I looked an idiot, again, only this time in front of lots of people who'd all spread the word that Poppy Saunders can't control her own pony. Even Hannah was looking a little impatient.

We took the next part of the ride steadily and Tanya rode next to me talking to me about being confident, and not giving in, and remembering to enjoy riding, and how lucky I was to have my own pony, and what a good pony Thunder was. It was all good advice. I nodded and smiled and she looked relieved.

"We'll just have a short canter before we get home," announced Tanya. "Not too fast, all right?" She looked at me as she said that and smiled reassuringly. "Okay, Poppy?"

I was so conscious of everyone watching me. How could I say no? That would spoil their morning and lead to more snickers and raised eyebrows. As it was, I was sure Tanya had kept the pace slow because of me up to now. I'd cantered lots of times, especially on Dandy. A mental picture of Dandy and me winning the bending race spurred me on. There he was now, ahead of me, being ridden by a boy named James, a boy six inches shorter and two years younger than I; no wonder I needed another pony.

The trail was wide and grassy, leading gently uphill, perfect for fast riding. I sat well into the saddle and tightened the reins as I kicked Thunder into a trot and then leaned forward slightly and kicked again. He sprinted ahead in a quick canter that took my breath away. It was really fun.

49

But then he accelerated again, treating the ride as a race, overtaking Socks, going faster than Dandy, faster than Smoke, faster than I'd ever gone before. We flashed past Tanya on Roland and I dimly heard her shout to me to slow Thunder down. I *was* trying to, but I'd lost both stirrups and I was hanging onto the reins for balance and fighting a losing battle.

The trail spiraled uphill into woods and became rougher underfoot. Thunder slowed instinctively and I tried to get back into the saddle and to pull the reins in, but he must have stumbled on a tree root. A sudden jerk threw me sideways and I slid until I was half lying with one leg over the saddle and the other bumping along the ground, the reins still somehow in my hands, twisting Thunder's head down and sideways too. Gradually but inevitably, gravity took me further down until my side hit the ground.

My panicky instinct to throw away the reins so as not to be dragged along helplessly proved unnecessary. Thunder had stopped and stood by me quietly, a picture of innocence.

If I could have made sure I never ever had to ride Thunder again, after that day, I'd have jumped at the chance. But that wasn't an option. No one took my fall at all seriously. I hadn't been hurt. Thunder had gone a little fast but he'd stopped.

I exaggerated the slight bruises I'd gotten and that got me a day or two off riding, and then I pretended to feel ill and spent several boring days lounging on a sofa at Hannah's house while the others were at the stables. Then Dad booked me an appointment at the doctor's and I had to get better fast before I was found out. It was all getting too silly now and out of control.

I tried talking about my worries to Hannah's mother. She was sympathetic, just like Tanya had been, and said she'd talk to Dad about my riding on Dandy again. But that didn't work. He seemed to have lost all patience with me, and got angry and said it was time I grew up a little and started confronting problems for myself. I knew deep down that he was right.

And Tanya seemed to be losing patience with me, too. I'm sure she felt I was making a small problem worse and, as far as she and everyone else was concerned, Thunder was a perfectly nice, well-behaved pony and I just had to learn to ride him. She was probably right, too.

To make things even worse, Ruby and Hannah were obviously fed up with me being a wimp. They were spending more and more time together and I missed out on the gossip and little jokes by not being there. I was really jealous, imagining them talking about me all the time, even when I didn't actually know they were. It was horrible. I spent hours alone inventing wild plans for becoming true friends with them again, and in particular to get Ruby to really like me again, but every time I actually tried to talk to them, the vexing subject of Thunder would come up, and we'd be on opposite sides.

Then I had an idea, out of the blue.

"I've been thinking," I said one night at supper.

Dad looked at me in a long-suffering kind of way. "About Thunder, I suppose? I'm not going to change my mind, Poppy. If Ruby had trouble with him, then you might have a case, but she's fine, and Tanya says the horse is fine, so I'm afraid you're just going to have to learn to cope."

"It wasn't about that," I said.

51

"What then?"

"Well ..." Now that it came to it, I was aware that I was proposing something quite momentous. "I thought, now that we're twelve, maybe it's time Ruby and I had separate rooms."

I didn't look at Ruby but I sensed her sit up and heard her yogurt spoon fall onto the table.

"Really?"

Dad sounded surprisingly pleased. I stole a glance at Ruby. She was stony-faced.

"I've been waiting for this," Dad went on. "Your mother and I talked a lot about how twins need to grow apart from each other. She did a lot of reading up about it. It's about each of you developing independent lives. I'm pleased, Poppy. Especially at the moment, when you haven't been showing your best side, it's good. Ruby, what do you think?"

The thing was, I believed I knew what Ruby would think. I was convinced she'd be devastated that I was choosing to separate us when life was already doing that to us for most of the daytime, at school and now during vacation. I was completely sure she'd protest; I imagined myself giving way to her pleas and us carrying on just as we'd always done, sharing our lives, telling each other everything. That was what I wanted her to say.

But Ruby didn't do any of that. She stared out of the window and nodded.

"Good idea," she said. "I've been thinking about it, too. Thanks, Dad."

And that was that.

The next morning was a Saturday. We spent most of it moving stuff in and out of bedrooms. Of course, as it had been my suggestion, I was the one who had to move into the old spare room. Dad was being so positive about it all, planning all that he'd have to buy in twos from now on, saying we could both have new comforters and curtains and stuff.

I tried to put on a brave face, and there was the advantage that there wasn't time to do much riding. Ruby still wasn't talking to me. She disappeared with Hannah mid-morning to exercise the ponies and for once Dad didn't nag at me to go, too, and the next day we visited our grandmother so that was another day off.

The nights were strange. We'd hardly ever spent a night apart, and it was so quiet without the noise of Ruby breathing or turning over or grunting. Dad checked on us both really sensitively, making sure we didn't regret the change. The trouble was, there was no way I was going to explain how I felt, and Ruby had withdrawn completely from communication. When Dad asked her, she said she was absolutely cool about it all. Cool was the word; she was as cold as ice. I couldn't even guess if she was telling the truth or not.

Chapter Five

After such an awful, lonely weekend, I was actually glad
to get down to the stables on Monday morning. I might not
have wanted to ride Thunder, but I still loved being among
all the ponies. Anyway, it was very busy, with lessons
booked all day long, so there was a lot I could do to help,
and no one seemed to notice that I wasn't actually riding.

After lunch a horse trailer trundled into the yard and
squealed to a stop. The driver got out and went over to
the ring, and a girl around our age jumped out eagerly and
looked around.

She looked nice; normal height, with very tanned
skin and shoulder-length blonde hair pushed back with a
headband. Her jeans were sloppy and patched and she had
on an old, faded sweatshirt. That made me warm up to her
right away. Ruby and Hannah were getting obsessive about
clothes and sometimes I longed to go back to the old days
when none of us cared what we looked like.

The new girl smiled at me as I slid off the fence where I'd been perched.

"Hi, I'm Poppy."

"Abi – Abigail. Do you live here?'

"No such luck, we live in the village. I haven't seen you around before, have I?"

"No, we've just moved here. Mom and Dad have arranged for me to keep Henry here – he's my pony. So we had to come right over."

Her father called to her and she went over to shake hands with Tanya, who saw me hovering.

"Poppy, this is Abigail. Can you help her unload her pony and then show her around while I finish this class? Just tie him up in the shade for a minute."

"Sure, I'd love to."

I said hello to Abi's father, and the three of us opened up the horse trailer. The most adorable pony was peering at us, long-lashed eyes peeping out from under a thick fringe of white mane. He was pale gold with a white splotch on his forehead, a long silky white mane and tail, and just a suspicion of feathers, long wisps of hair sprouting from his pasterns and covering the top of his hooves.

"He's beautiful!"

"I know, I just love him to bits. He's special, too; he's a Haflinger."

"I know he comes from Austria," I said.

"Wow, you must be an expert. No one's ever heard of Haflingers, usually."

"I read a lot about ponies," I explained, "and there was a book about pony breeds that I read not long ago. I remember liking how hairy they are."

"Me too. So cuddly."

"If you two have stopped talking about him, can we get unloaded?" said Abi's dad, in a nice way. "I've got a houseful of furniture to get unpacked."

"Sorry!" we said in unison, swapping a grin. I'm going to like Abi, I thought.

Abi untied him and he backed out easily, clattering noisily down the ramp and looking around at his new home in an easy, confident way. I remembered how fidgety Thunder had been the first day and wished with all my heart that Dad had chosen a pony like Henry for us.

"Okay if I leave you for now and go and help Mom with the house?" Abi's Dad asked.

"I'll be fine."

"I'll look after her," I volunteered eagerly.

The horse trailer backed out carefully; Henry was completely unperturbed, of course. We tethered him under a big oak tree and then I showed Abi around the whole place: the stable block, the tack room, Tanya's house, the paddock where the ponies spend the night and where there are some cross country jumps, and the enclosed ring where Tanya was teaching. We leaned on the fence companionably and ate some of the chocolate she produced while we talked. Her new house was just down the road from ours, and in September she'd be coming to the same school as us.

"What grade will you be in?"

"Eighth; I turned twelve in January. How about you?"

"The same. Isn't that great? We were twelve a month ago, at the start of the vacation, and our best friend's going to be twelve in two weeks."

"You said we?" Abi looked puzzled.

"Didn't I mention it? I'm a twin."

"Oh, how exciting! I've never really known twins before. Do you look exactly the same?"

"No, we're not identical. We're more like normal brothers and sisters, just with the same birthday," I explained.

"Well, I've got an older brother. He's sixteen, and most of the time we fight. He's got some really strange ideas. It must be much nicer being a twin. I suppose you do everything together?"

She looked around as if to see if my twin was there. Until recently, she probably would've been.

I shrugged. "Mostly we do things together but we share a pony so it's not so easy."

"Have you got your own pony, too? That's great! What's his name?"

I told her a little about Thunder, what he looked like and how he'd been a surprise present, trying to sound positive.

"I've had Henry for nearly a year," Abi said, "and before that I knew him because he was owned by an older boy at the riding school I used to go to. It was fantastic to know he was mine, of course, but it wasn't as exciting as what happened to you."

"No, I suppose not."

I heard voices and hooves and turned to see Hannah and Ruby riding back into the yard; they must have been riding down the trail.

"Here they are," I said, not wildly enthusiastic at the idea of sharing Abi with them.

"Okay, let me guess which one's your twin." Abi stared solemnly as the girls dismounted and started running up stirrups and stuff. "The one with the braid?"

"Nope, that's Hannah. Ruby, Hannah – come and meet Abi. She's just arrived with Henry."

"Henry? Who's Henry?" asked Ruby, looking around. That's one of the things I'd noticed had changed about her recently; she was much too interested in boys.

Abi laughed. "That's Henry." She pointed to where he was standing patiently, tail swishing gently, watching this new world all around him.

"He's so sweet!" Both girls rushed over to say hello, pulling Socks and Thunder along behind them. Thunder snorted indignantly and pulled back against the reins, so Ruby thrust them into my hands.

"You tie him up, Poppy," she said over her shoulder.

"Come on then," I muttered to my pony, who gave me his usual supercilious look, as though he found me really boring. I untacked him and was just about to turn him out into the paddock when Ruby, Hannah and Abi came swooping over to inspect him and Socks.

"You didn't say what a beauty he is," commented Abi, stroking Thunder's neck. He nuzzled her hand in a trusting way.

"He's really fast," boasted Ruby. "We were cantering just now..." She stopped to check that Tanya was out of earshot, "... we had a race, and Socks is really, really fast, but Thunder won."

"I bet he did. You can see how strong he is," said Abi admiringly. "But Socks is gorgeous, too. He's such a lovely color. Have you ever noticed, his tail's –"

"Exactly the same color as Hannah's hair!" Ruby and I chorused together, and for a moment the tensions of the last few weeks disappeared as we shared our old joke.

"Oh, look, Henry and Socks are making friends," said Hannah. She'd left Socks loose. He'd wandered across to Henry and the two ponies were sniffing each other companionably.

"I'll take Thunder over and let him join in," suggested Ruby, grabbing his head collar from me. The three girls and three ponies gathered in a friendly bunch. Thunder might just as well have not been my pony at all. And the trouble was, I couldn't decide if that was a good or bad idea.

Tanya arrived just then, the lesson over, and told Hannah and Ruby to turn Thunder and Socks out into the paddock.

"We'll put Henry into a box for now, as we did with Thunder at the start," she said. "The one next to where he's been. Poppy, can you just do me a favor and make sure it's ready?"

Pleased to be given a job, since she didn't seem to want to ask me to deal with Thunder, I ran ahead and opened the door. There was clean, fresh bedding on the floor and plenty of water, and I went to the feed room to get a hay net.

I lugged it in and hung it on the wall, just as Abi led Henry in.

"Right, let's leave him alone for some peace and quiet after the excitement of his long journey," said Tanya. "And isn't it time you all went home for lunch?"

"Come with us, Abi?" suggested Ruby.

"If I'm allowed to; it's chaos at home, I bet."

"Let's go that way home and ask," I said.

"Good thinking." Hannah linked her arm with mine and we led the way, along the lane, past her house and on to the newly built house where a big furniture van was unloading furniture. Abi's preoccupied parents said yes, of course, that she could spend the rest of the afternoon with us, and out from under their feet. So back to Hannah's we went, for pizza and ice cream and lots of talk and laughter and fun.

Black Monday had transformed itself into quite a hopeful day, after all.

○ ○ ○ ○

It didn't take long for Abi to work out that I had a problem
with Thunder. Unlike the other two, she seemed able
to understand a little better where I was coming from.
Although she'd been riding for three years, she was, like
me, not particularly brave or competitive either.

Soon, Henry joined the other ponies in the paddock.
Thunder spent his nights there now, too. We got into an
easy routine of meeting either at Hannah's house or at
Abi's, and then going down to the stables for most of
the day, which was just like before except that now I
sometimes rode Henry and the other three would swap
around, although Abi avoided Thunder after he stopped
at a jump and nearly threw her off.

Of course, I couldn't ride Henry very often, but when
I did it was so nice, just like being on a bigger version
of Dandy. He was very obedient and placid, and needed
waking up a little sometimes, but I always felt with him
that I was in the driver's seat, whereas when I was riding
Thunder he did more or less what he wanted, unless Tanya,
whom he respected, was there.

So when we had our lessons, I rode Thunder for the
minimum time possible, and most days I got a quick ride
on Henry. Still I didn't go trail riding with the others, and
when we spent long afternoons messing around in the
paddock, one of us had to be the non-rider in all the games
and competitions we devised, and that one was almost
always me.

Abi and I got along really well, but that meant Ruby and
Hannah still spent a lot of time with their heads together,
giggling and sharing secrets, the way you do with a best
friend. Every night at home, when we went to bed, I hoped

Ruby would come into my new room, to gossip and to share worries the way we'd always done, but she was still withdrawn where I was concerned. I tried talking to her about it, and even started to explain why I'd suggested the separate room thing in the first place, but I got nowhere. It was like talking to a brick wall.

"You two don't seem that close for twins," Abi observed curiously one day.

"I suppose we aren't any more. We used to be ..."

"That's growing up," she said wisely. "Well, I'm glad, because it means we can be friends."

"That's true."

I was happy about what she said, but I felt sad at the same time.

Hannah's birthday was going to be the big party that summer. She'd been allowed to invite lots of friends for a barbecue and dancing in the evening, and during the day her parents arranged for the four of us to have the use of the riding school for gymkhana games for a couple of hours, all by ourselves.

The day before, we sprawled under a tree in Hannah's yard to make plans.

"Are we going to have a sudden death tournament or what?" Ruby asked.

"Definitely sudden death," agreed Hannah, who was almost as fixated on winning as Ruby. "We can draw up a schedule, like a proper gymkhana."

"Yes, but if it's too serious, you two'll win right from the start and Abi and I won't have anything to do," I objected.

Ruby shrugged. "That's up to you. No one's going to *make* you lose. You don't mind, do you, Abi?"

"Yes, you want to win, don't you?" added Hannah. "It'll be serious fun."

"Well, yes." Abi looked a little embarrassed, glancing from them to me.

Ruby sighed in a long-suffering kind of way. "Maybe we should cut out the sudden death idea, just for Poppy?"

I glared at her.

"I'll ask Mom to make us a picnic lunch, if you like," offered Abi. She was good at changing the subject like that, when things got tense between Ruby and me.

"As well as the barbecue?"

"Why not? We're sure to be starving." She picked up a third muffin from the plate that lay between us.

"You won't be if you eat all those," observed Ruby.

"They're my favorites!" she protested.

"I'll have an apple. I can't afford to get fat."

"I'm not fat!" Abi squealed and threw herself at Ruby. They tussled together, rolling over and over in the long grass, giggling.

Eventually they calmed down and we carried on.

"Well, I think the picnic's a great idea," said Hannah, "and it's my birthday, so that's decided."

"We'll need special treats for the ponies, too," I added.

"I suppose you'll be rationing what Thunder gets," said Ruby, suddenly turning on me again.

"I thought I'd starve him, actually," I said airily.

"*Poor* Thunder, it's lucky for him he's got me to look after him."

"Oh yeah?" I flared up. "So who is it who does most of the grooming, then?"

"Don't you dare suggest I don't do my share!" she countered fiercely.

62

"Do you? I hadn't noticed."

"Stop it, you two!" Hannah pushed between us and eyeballed each of us in turn. "This is completely stupid. And it's *my* birthday we're supposed to be celebrating."

"And it's *my* pony that she doesn't *ever* want to ride," said Ruby, making a face at me.

I stuck my tongue out at her. I couldn't actually think of any better retort, because some of what she was accusing me of was true.

Abi tried to intervene. "That's a mean thing to say, Ruby. You know Poppy does her fair share of looking after Thunder, even when she hasn't been out on him. After all, Thunder definitely belongs to both of you, doesn't he?"

Ruby shrugged. "In theory, but we all know what Poppy's like with him."

There was a pause. All three of them were looking at me in a pitying kind of way.

"If only Dad had let us choose –" I started to say.

Hannah intervened. "You know what, Poppy, there's a saying that fits you perfectly. "Don't look a gift horse in the mouth.""

"And what's that mean?" asked Abi, looking blank.

"Don't you know? It means, don't say no to a present even when it's not exactly what you want. Your Dad bought the best pony he could. Thunder's yours, so enjoy him!"

Ruby jumped up and stood over me. "It's not just that, though, is it, Poppy?" She took a deep breath. "We've all agreed already that Poppy's lost her nerve – that is, if she ever had a nerve in the first place."

There was a general gasp, as if they were all three shocked that the cat had finally been let out of the bag. So, they'd been talking about me when they were out riding

63

together and they'd worked it out that I was a total coward.

The trouble was, where Thunder was concerned, and Socks too, it was all too true. Yet I knew I'd be fine if only I could ride a pony like Henry or Dandy, and take my time.

I had to defend myself somehow. "Just because I don't want to win all the time!" I protested angrily.

"All the time? Never!"

"All right, that's it! Either you two shut up, or you can both go home and miss everything and Abi and I will do my party on our own." Hannah looked so fierce that we both took deep breaths and simmered down. Ruby glared at me, clenching her fists, and I half longed to hit her and half wanted to hug her and make up. I looked deep into my twin's eyes, searching for the sister and friend who I'd shared all those years with, but it was like looking at a stranger.

What was going on between us?

"Say sorry to each other," suggested Abi. "That's what Mom makes my brother and me do. You don't actually have to mean it," she added helpfully.

"Go on, this is horrible," said Hannah, touching each of us with a pleading hand.

"Sorry, Ruby," I said, pretty much at the same instant that she said sorry to me, and probably with as little conviction.

Ruby looked tearful and Abi handed her a tissue sympathetically.

"Let's forget all this nonsense and get on with my birthday plans," insisted Hannah. "Ruby, why don't you and I do the competition plan and then Abi can help Poppy get all the stuff we need?"

"Oh no, don't leave me out of the scheduling; that's what I like best," interrupted Abi.

"Well, can you get the stuff on your own, Poppy?"

"Sure. Whatever you all decide." I know I sounded really sulky, but the argument had really shocked me.

I sat on the edge of the group, feeling that no one was very interested in what I might have to say, since I'd probably not be riding much, listening to the increasingly complicated preparations. Ruby and Hannah created a massive list of races and games, including what seemed like a terrifyingly hard jumping course, and Abi suggested extra games from her old riding school.

"The best one ever was a dress-up race," she said eagerly.

"That doesn't sound too challenging," said Ruby, dismissively.

"It depends on the clothes," Abi explained.

"It would be fun," I said, speaking for the first time for a long time. Maybe this was a race I could do just as well as the others.

"Poppy, you've got that massive dress-up box at your house from when we were little, haven't you? We used to have the best games, Abi." Hannah gave me a hug.

Ruby looked at the other two. She must've noticed how they were supporting me, so she changed tack. "While you're at it, Poppy, why don't you see if there are any sacks lying around the tack room? There should be some from that day at the start of vacation."

"I'll see what I can find. What else?"

"Eggs and spoons; have you got any eggs at home?" asked Hannah.

"Lots," I said. It was so nice to be part of the

conversation again. "Dad has this theory we should eat eggs for breakfast but neither of us likes them so there're millions of eggs sitting around going stale."

"You'll have to hard boil them," said Abigail. "Just think of the mess otherwise ..."

"Only if you drop your egg, which the good riders won't."

"Don't be mean, Ruby," I said, going red.

"I didn't mean to be," she said quickly. "Look, let's make a list."

When the long list was ready at last, I went to ask Hannah's mother if I could go home alone. Dad would be back soon, and anyway we were being given lots more freedom all that summer; it was one of the better things about growing up. Our village is totally safe, once you're old enough to know not to throw yourself under a passing truck.

First, though, I ran back to the stables and fished through the bits and pieces that were piled up at the back of the tack room and found all sorts of stuff for games, including the flags we must have been using the day Dandy and I won our race.

I slipped down to sit against the wall and remembered what fun it had been and how unclouded the future had felt, just before Thunder arrived. Eyes closed, I re-lived the race back and forth, faster and faster, and wondered why I was so frightened of going fast and jumping on Thunder when I'd been able to do all that on Dandy. The tack room was always cozy, and the sharp smell of leather and metal polish mixed with the warmth of the room made me feel quite emotional, thinking about the way things had been.

I heard footsteps and jumped up, wiping my wet eyes with the back of my hand.

"I didn't know you were here, Poppy," Tanya said. "Are you all right?"

"Mmmm. We've been planning tomorrow afternoon. Can we borrow all this stuff?"

"As long as it all goes back, yes. Are you going to be jumping?"

"I think so. They're talking about putting up a course."

"I meant you, Poppy. Are you going to have a try?"

I felt myself go red.

"I'm not sure," I mumbled.

"Poppy, you really are going to have to pull yourself together," Tanya said. "It's not helping anyone, especially not you, being so silly about Thunder."

I'd been right; she'd lost sympathy with me.

"If you say so," I said defensively. "Can I go now? I've got lots of stuff to get together for tomorrow."

"Take care," she said automatically. "Off you go."

I could feel her watching me as I ran off.

Chapter Six

It took forever to find enough clothes for the dress-up race, as there had to be four of everything, and then I had to boil four eggs, and find spoons, and balloons left over from our last party, and some large potatoes. Dad got home in the middle of it all and was full of enthusiasm. He found a box of chocolates for the first prize and gave me some money to spend on more prizes and on nice pony treats like pony nuts which I could buy at the stables the next day.

By now I was full of excitement. I made a solemn promise to myself that this was when everything was going to change. This time I'd ride my own pony and do all the games and even try the jumping course, and everyone would truly like me again, and not treat me as if I was totally useless.

When Ruby got back, she seemed to have put our fight behind her. We talked nonstop about the following day and managed to forget our differences for once. Dad joined in and suggested extraordinary and impractical new games, but in the most lovable way. It was the nicest evening I'd spent since Thunder arrived. Maybe things were looking up?

When we went up to bed, we drifted in and out of each other's rooms and it began to feel like old times. I was just about to suggest I drag my mattress into our old bedroom so we could keep on chatting when the phone rang. It was Hannah, wanting to talk through more plans with Ruby, and they got totally engrossed, and talked for a long time.

In the end, I got into bed as usual, and hoped Ruby would come in after she'd finished with Hannah, and tell me all about it.

But she didn't.

The next morning, we had to do jobs around the house and yard with Dad before we were allowed to go down to the stables, and we also had to pack our overnight stuff as Abi and we would be sleeping over at Hannah's house after the barbecue. It was a lovely sunny day, with little white clouds scudding along in the breeze, which was just strong enough to keep it from being too hot, so we wore jodhpurs and T-shirts and took shorts to change into for the evening.

"Don't you think you should take jackets?" Dad said, fussing over us and making sure we'd packed our toothbrushes.

"In this weather? We'll be fine!"

"Make sure you've put in clean underwear for the morning."

"Yes, Dad," we chorused.

Dad was always very careful that when we went to a sleepover we had everything right. I think it was because he was aware of being a single father and wanted to do everything that mothers do properly. He was being so much nicer now that he thought I was happier with Thunder; and the only reason he thought that was because there was a conspiracy of silence going on between Ruby, Tanya and me, and all for different motives.

After lunch he walked down to the stables with us and said he'd drop off our overnight bag at Hannah's.

"I'll just take a look at my investment," he said, wandering over to the paddock. "Go and catch him, Poppy."

I knew he was testing me, but luckily for me catching Thunder wasn't an issue, now that I was used to him. He wasn't always the easiest pony to catch, actually, since he liked to canter off just when you put your hand on his head collar, but that was mischief rather than malice, and I knew how to deal with that. I made sure I had some sugar lumps in my hand; I always kept a few in a little box in the tack room. So I shot off there first, and then strolled through the paddock, saying hello to my favorite ponies, like Dandy and Henry, and eventually when I got near Thunder I clicked my tongue and got his attention. I held out my hand with a sugar lump balanced on it, and he sauntered over and lapped it up. Then while he was crunching, I grabbed his head collar and led him back to the fence.

"Good girl," Dad said, leaning over to stroke Thunder's long thin nose. "I can see you're not at all frightened of him anymore. Have a great day today, won't you? I'm going to spend the night away; there's a big golf game tomorrow morning so I'm staying with a friend. That's okay with you both, isn't it?"

"We'll be fine."

"Have a nice time. Don't forget to win!" That was said to Ruby, of course.

"Okay, let's get going," she said as soon as Dad had gone. "I've got to set up the jumps now that the morning classes are over. Can you get the race stuff?"

"No problem, I've put it all together in the tack room, and Dad's given me money to spend on pony treats, so I'll talk to Tanya about that. Oh, look, what *has* Abi brought?"

Abi was staggering under the weight of a massive basket.

"It's the picnic," she shouted as she got nearer. "Mom let me choose whatever we wanted, so I brought a little of everything."

"You certainly did," said Ruby, laughing. "There can't be much left at home."

"And Mom baked a cake for Hannah, too."

Abi squatted down by the basket and opened a container; inside was an iced birthday cake complete with twelve candles.

"Wow, and she's getting the same again this evening!" I said.

Abi looked a little annoyed. "I didn't think she'd mind. I wouldn't. You've all become such good friends, and I'm so lucky to have found you."

"I didn't mean it like that," I said, although actually I sort of did think it was all too much, and I bet Ruby was thinking the same, though true to form she wasn't going to admit it if it meant agreeing with me.

At any rate, the awkward moment passed and soon Hannah arrived, wearing brand-new jodhpurs and a cool designer T-shirt.

We gave her presents; Abi's was the picnic, and a book showing different horse breeds. The Haflinger wasn't half as pretty as Henry. Ruby and I had bought her separate presents, something we'd never done before. Mine was a

71

framed photo of a horse that looked a little like Socks and Ruby's was accessories – a bracelet and earrings. I thought that was sort of a strange present for someone as pony-crazy as Hannah, but she seemed to like it a lot.

The other three started putting up the jumps while I put all the game stuff in heaps so we could move quickly from one competition to the other. Tanya hovered about and checked to make sure everything was safe, lowering two of the five jumps and reducing the spread of the double. That cheered me up, as I was more than a little worried about the jumping.

Then we were ready to start.

We tacked up the ponies and Ruby stuck the schedule up on the stable wall. It was long and complicated with about twenty different events, but what I noticed was that each time, each pony was put down only once. That was logical, of course, but it hadn't really registered with me before that Ruby and I would have to share the riding, as usual, rather than each having a try at each event. There was going to be a lot of hanging around while the others were riding.

"Ruby and Poppy, you need to work out who's doing what," said Hannah, obviously thinking the same thing.

Ruby looked at me and waited, and I knew, of course, that she wanted to do as much as she possibly could. Did I dare suggest I do the jumping? Why not? Thunder was mine as much as hers, and I'd made myself that solemn promise. What was the worst that could happen? I'd fall off ... so what? I took a deep breath and opened my mouth, but at the last minute the words changed themselves.

"I'll do the flag race," I said.

"Sure, and I'll do the jumping, if you like," Ruby said casually but not in a way that gave me an option to object.

That was it, then. I'd psyched myself up to this being the moment when everything would suddenly go right, like at the gymkhana at the start of the summer, and now I wouldn't even have a try at jumping.

"Why don't you ride Henry in the potato race?" Abi offered.

"You can try Socks again if you feel like it," said Hannah.

I shook my head. I felt flattened, deflated. All the confidence I'd been building up just trickled away.

"Thanks, Hannah, but no. It'll be nice to have a turn on Henry once or twice, though."

"What else do you want Thunder for? Bending? Fancy Dress?" asked Ruby carelessly, not looking at me.

"There's a Chase-me-Charlie. The fence'll start low," suggested Abi, kindly.

My stomach went wobbly as I imagined myself racing the others and the fence getting higher each time. It was no use, I'd have to drop out.

"I tell you what, Ruby," I said, "why don't you do the first few events on Thunder, and I'll take over when he gets tired."

I could feel all three of them looking at me as if to say, what a loser, and they shrugged in unison.

"You can be in charge of scoring," Hannah suggested, kindly.

I nodded. I was going to be an outsider, just as I had been for the last few weeks, and I couldn't honestly say it was anyone's fault but mine.

I'm sure the others would say it was a great afternoon. The sun shone, we had the whole riding school to ourselves, and although Tanya hovered, she stayed in the background and let us do our own thing as long as we were safe. If only I'd been riding Dandy, it would've been perfect.

I watched the jumping and kept score. Ruby did a perfect round on Thunder, looking entirely at one with him as they lifted and landed sweetly for each of the jumps. I clapped and whooped with the others, and wished it had been me.

After Hannah and Abi finished their rounds, Ruby looked guilty and said, "It's not fair that you haven't had a turn, Poppy; we should have sorted it differently."

"You're right, we didn't think it through," said Hannah. "Go on, Poppy."

I hesitated.

"Have a try," said Abi.

They were my friends, after all. They wanted me to be part of the group, and the only way that would happen would be if I joined in. I just had to pull myself together.

Half happy and half terrified, I scrambled onto Thunder and walked him into the ring. The jumps looked much bigger than the ones I'd been used to on Dandy; well, they could be, as all three of our ponies were bigger. I don't think anyone realized I'd never actually jumped Thunder; I'd gotten so good at avoiding riding him.

I fiddled with the stirrup leathers to put off the terrifying moment of starting, but I couldn't delay forever.

"Go on!" shouted Ruby, impatiently. "Don't take all day."

I glared at her and she glared back.

All right. This would have to be it.

I gripped the reins as tightly as I could and trotted Thunder toward the first jump. He pulled, trying to extend his head, and I instinctively pulled against him, leaning back in the saddle. But as we approached, he wrenched

74

the reins through my fingers and took off in his own style, jumping high and freely, clearing the cross bar easily. He landed with a bump that bounced me sideways and carried straight on toward the next jump.

"Well done!" "Great stuff!" "Fantastic!" I could vaguely hear the others encouraging me, but I wasn't registering any of it. I knew I hadn't had anything to do with Thunder clearing the jump, and more importantly, it soon became obvious I didn't have a hope of staying on for the next one. He accelerated into a fast canter, threw himself at the obstacle with wild enthusiasm, leaving me quite literally behind. As he landed on the far side, I was already lying spread-eagled on the ground on the takeoff side.

"Are you okay?" Abi came running toward me and hauled me up.

"I think so ..."

Ruby came over, leading Thunder. His eyes were excited and bright and he looked full of energy.

"Up you go," she said. "You're not hurt, are you?"

"No." It was true, I'd slid off gently and only my pride had been damaged. "I don't think I'll do any more for now, though."

I could see the scorn in her eyes.

"That wasn't a bad fall, Poppy." Tanya had run over to check me out. "You know what you're supposed to do – get back on and try again, right away. That way you stay confident and the pony knows who's boss."

She looked a little uncertain as she said that, because clearly I wasn't confident and Thunder was definitely the boss.

I shook my head firmly.

Hannah and Abi were really nice. They pleaded with me to have another try, but I was determined not to.

Ruby just looked blank. Eventually she shrugged as if in despair and said, "Oh well, I'll just take him around the jumps once more to make sure he's okay."

"If you're going to have another turn, so are we!" shrieked Hannah excitedly.

So all three of them did another round, and by then Thunder and Socks were tied for first place, so they did one more round and Socks was the overall winner. Ruby wasn't too thrilled about that.

I just stood around watching and entered the scores onto the sheet. Right at the end, Abi ran over and offered me a try on Henry, and I nearly said yes, but it was too late; the other two were already dismantling the course and shouting for me to get the obstacle race ready.

I felt massively relieved that all those looming fences were gone; surely, even I could do gymkhana games. I screwed my fingers tightly so that my nails dug into my palms and gritted my teeth. I just wasn't going to let myself panic and cop out again. The long list of events fluttered in the breeze and I imagined how good it would be when all the games had happened and the long afternoon was finally over.

I felt better when we got on with preparing for the games and everyone was asking me where things were and being nice about all the stuff I'd gotten ready in advance. There was a welcome delay, too, as the ponies needed a rest, so we attacked the picnic. It was delicious, but massive, and a little heavy with a barbecue looming. Tanya joined us for some cake and kept looking at me, as if she was going to say something and then stopping herself, but I tried not to meet her eyes.

Then we started the games.

Or at least, the others did. I just don't know what happened to me. When Abi offered me Henry for the potato race, I said no. Even when she said I could ride him in the fancy dress race, which was a total riot and very funny, I said no. And when it was my turn to ride Thunder in the flag race, the last of the afternoon and the only one that I was definitely booked to do, I pretended I'd twisted my ankle and said Ruby could ride after all.

"Poor you," she said perfunctorily as she turned Thunder back to the others. I knew she didn't believe me.

I felt slightly sick from too much cake and sick with myself too. I knew I was being ridiculous and yet I just didn't seem able to do anything about it.

"Not riding much?" Tanya remarked casually as she wandered by to check on us.

"Not much," I said, head down, staring at the score sheet.

She stood by me for a minute as if she was waiting for me to say something, and then, when I didn't, she walked away.

The races finished with a complicated ceremony that Hannah and Ruby had apparently devised the night before, when they were on the phone for so long. It involved each rider and pony doing a series of maneuvers: Around the World, vaulting onto the saddle, trying to swing under the saddle and back again, that sort of thing. Then there was a mad gallop around the ring all together. Of course, I wasn't part of that but at the end I was called into the ring to present Dad's box of chocolates to Hannah, who'd gotten the highest number of points, and two bars of chocolate to the other two, and a handful of pony nuts for each of the ponies.

"And three cheers for Abi's mother for the picnic!" Ruby shouted excitedly.

"And three cheers for Tanya for letting us ride here all afternoon!" yelled Abi.

I joined in, of course.

After that, we had to untack and rub down the ponies, turn them out, and tidy up which took a long time and got quite boring, especially as I spent most of the time on my own, collecting scattered fancy dresses and scavenging for potatoes and stuff. Not only that, but the other three were endlessly swapping stories about the afternoon.

We finally got back to Hannah's, where her dad was getting stressed about the barbecue that wouldn't light. The whole yard stank of lighter fluid. Hannah's mother noticed me skulking around in the background and asked me kindly how the afternoon had gone but it was the last thing I wanted to talk about. A little pity and I knew I'd burst into tears and make a total fool of myself. I pretended my ankle was hurting, and she gave me a warm drink and suggested I go inside and watch TV for a while, which got me away from the others and gave me a chance to calm down. Once all the other guests had arrived and the tantalizing smell of burgers and hot dogs started to waft in through the open window, I pulled myself together and went outside. I knew almost all of Hannah's friends, and luckily quite a lot of them didn't ride, so I actually had fun talking and eating and playing silly games and dancing.

Still, I couldn't forget the afternoon. It had been the very disaster I had dreaded.

Chapter Seven

It was after everyone had gone home that the real trouble began.

The four of us got changed and squashed our sleeping bags together on the floor of Hannah's bedroom.

"Why doesn't one of you use the bed?" Hannah's dad asked in a bemused sort of way when he stuck his head in the doorway to say goodnight. We just giggled. He sighed, turned the light off and shut the door.

"As if we'd want to be in a silly bed," said Hannah.

"This is much more fun," Ruby added, stretching her arms and bashing me on the ear. "Oh, sorry, Poppy."

"That's okay," I mumbled, shifting around on the hard floor and wondering whether the bed might not be a better option after all. "Hey, that was a great barbecue, Hannah."

"The best," said Abi. "And look, I've brought up some chips and a bottle of soda so we can carry on all night."

"Midnight feast!" yelled Ruby enthusiastically.

"Shhh," hissed Hannah. "Mom'll hear and she'll never let us, not after all the food we've had today already."

"She could be right," I said, rubbing my stomach, which felt pretty swollen with all the burgers and chips and cake and stuff that it was still trying to digest.

"Spoil sport," said Ruby, scornfully, "always trying to ruin our fun."

"That's not fair!" I sat up and hit my head against Abi's elbow.

"Ouch!"

"Sorry!"

"That reminds me, how's your ankle?" Hannah asked. "I forgot all about it."

"You didn't have much problem dancing," remarked Abi. "It got better really fast."

"If you ever twisted it at all," Ruby said almost casually. "I sometimes wonder why you bother with riding at all anymore. After all, as I said before, you've completely lost your nerve."

There was a stunned silence.

"That's a little harsh," Hannah said, eventually. "I mean, just because Poppy didn't want to jump today ..."

"Or ride in any of the races, and not just on Thunder. You said no to Henry, too, didn't you?"

My sister's face loomed through the darkness and glared at me.

Why was she being so cruel? What had I done to her?

I gulped but I couldn't think of anything to say.

Abi came to my defense.

"She's probably a little tired," she said, lamely. "I know I was by the end. It's not easy riding a strange pony when you're tired."

"Henry's not exactly strange, though, is he?" commented Hannah, sounding puzzled. "You've ridden him a lot. What's really going on, Poppy?"

They'd all three sat up now and were surrounding me; even though it was dark, I could feel them. Normally that would have been comforting, but at the moment it felt horrible and threatening. I still didn't know what to say.

"You see, she *has* lost her nerve," said Ruby. "She can't even talk to us anymore, and we're supposed to be her best friends."

"It's not that," I managed to say, though my throat was all swollen with tears.

"Riding's so much fun!" said Abi. "You're missing out, Poppy, it's silly."

"And you don't know how lucky you are with Thunder. We all envy you, he's such a good jumper. You should be so proud of him," added Hannah.

"Tell us what the problem is." Abi put her arm around my shoulders comfortingly.

There was a long silence. I sniffed hard and tried not to cry, but I couldn't stop a big sob that echoed around the room.

"He's so big," I gulped, pathetically. I hated myself at that moment.

There was a long silence. Then Ruby broke it.

"Oh, for goodness sake. Why don't you just admit that you're not really a rider? Let's be honest, you've always been kinda wimpy, but now it's gotten to the stage when you might as well admit the truth and tell Dad you want a bike or swimming lessons or whatever, and leave the rest of us to get on with our lives."

"Maybe she's right," Hannah said, not cruelly, but

practically. "After all, if you don't want to ride, there's not much point in having a pony, is there?"

"She likes being at the stables," Abi said, sticking up for me again.

I was just watching them, like I was watching a TV show about myself.

"Yes, but that's not *riding*. You don't need your own pony to be a stable hand." Ruby's tone was so offhand, it made me shake off my misery and become angry instead, even with Hannah and Abi who were being nice to me. I sat up straight and shrugged off Abi's arm.

"I just want to be left alone, okay?" I shouted. "So maybe I don't want to be a great rider, or win competitions, or anything. Maybe I'd prefer to do ballet or something. Maybe ..."

The door flew open. Hannah's mother was standing there, looking really annoyed.

"Girls! What on earth's going on? This is meant to be a fun sleepover, not a shouting match. Poppy, what are you screaming about?"

"They're all giving me a hard time," I started, but Hannah's mother cut me off.

"It sounds as if you're all being horrible to each other. Well, I can't send you and Ruby home, Poppy, since your dad's away, but one more squeak out of any of you and you'll all be in big trouble. Understood?"

We all nodded silently. My heart was pounding with a mix of fury and guilt, and misery.

"Does anyone need to tell me anything before you all settle down?"

I opened my mouth but I saw the other three looking at me. How could I snitch on my closest friends? If I moaned any more, that could be the very end of the friendship between us; even between my twin and me. I couldn't do that, I didn't want to do that. I shut my mouth tight.

"Goodnight then."

The door swung shut and there was a stifled giggle from Abi.

"It's not funny!" hissed Ruby.

"I know. I'm sorry, I couldn't help it. She was so stressed."

"Don't you dare laugh at me!"

"Not you, Poppy, Hannah's mother. Of course, you weren't exactly ..."

"Just shut up, all of you," Hannah whispered fiercely. "Just go to sleep and maybe tomorrow we can sort this all out."

There was a long silence, as if we were all holding our breath.

Then the whispering and hysterical giggling started again, but I kept out of it. They had to quiet down when Hannah's parents went to bed, but then they started again. I tried telling them to shush, but that just made things worse. Ruby made snide comments about my being a goody-goody, and this time the others must have had enough of me being such a pain and went along with her.

Eventually, bit-by-bit, they shuffled into comfortable positions and dropped off to sleep. Hannah dragged her comforter onto the bed, away from us. Abi's breathing lengthened as she went to sleep, and eventually the other two stopped fidgeting and went quiet, too.

I couldn't sleep, though. The events of the last couple of days whirled around and around in my head: the arguments, the party, Ruby and me having fun last night at home, falling off Thunder because I was such a bad rider, being alone. Most of all, I kept trying to work out why I hadn't been able to ride even in the easy gymkhana games. What had stopped me when I thought I'd made up my mind? Were the others right? Had I really lost my nerve for riding, and should I just give up forever? And, if that were true, how would I explain it to Dad, who hates cowards? How could I ever expect him to feel the same way about me again?

Ruby coughed once or twice in her sleep, the way she does, and I felt a tug as if my heart would break. That sounds melodramatic, but it truly did feel like that. How on earth could we make things right between us ever again?

The long night dragged on. An owl hooted somewhere and a dog barked every now and then. I pictured the ponies out in their paddock, sleeping upright but relaxed with one rear leg bent. That made me think about Thunder. He'd be just like the others, peaceful and quiet, not frightening or aggressive as I often imagined him. Just a nice pony. My pony. Our pony.

I crawled out of my sleeping bag and crept over to the window. The moon was out, and I could see Hannah's yard all ghostly in the strange light, and a field beyond, its boundaries all blurred, and then the night sky, with stars everywhere. I leaned my forehead against the cool glass and tried to think things through logically. I didn't really want to stop riding. I certainly didn't want to lose my friends. I wanted Ruby and Dad to like me as well as love me. So, I needed to take control of my fears, to do something about the ridiculous situation I'd gotten myself into. To prove myself. But how? What could I do?

And then it came to me. I would sneak out as soon as it got light, go down to the stables, and take Thunder out all by myself. Not just for a quick ride, but for a long day's ride. Alone.

I took a deep breath. It might be a disaster. Or, it might, just, sort me out for good.

I didn't mean to, of course, but I fell asleep, squashed uncomfortably between the window wall and the foot of Hannah's bed, and when I woke suddenly, I thought I'd missed my chance. Bright sunlight was streaming into the room and all the birds were singing. Yet the other three were still asleep, and when I'd maneuvered myself past all the bodies to where we'd dumped our clothes and found my watch, it only said six o'clock. Not as early as I'd planned, but, with luck, early enough.

We'd changed clothes for the party and Hannah's mother had put our jodhpurs and boots away somewhere so I'd have to ride in shorts and sneakers; at least it didn't look cold outside. I got dressed as quietly as I could and tiptoed downstairs. The front door squeaked as I opened it and I waited on tenterhooks for someone to wake up, but only the cat came and pressed herself against my legs, hoping breakfast had come early.

That made me stop. Food. I didn't have any money, and if I was going to be out all day I'd need something to eat. I could take something from Hannah's kitchen, but even though we spent so much time at her house, that felt a little like stealing. I decided to try our own house. I slipped through Hannah's front door and closed it carefully behind me. There. I couldn't go back now without complicated explanations. I'd have to follow my plan.

The village was silent; it was a Sunday so no one was

rushing off to work early. I ran along to our house and opened the door with the key that Ruby and I shared.

It felt strange being alone in our house; I'm not sure I'd ever been completely on my own there before. Even though Dad sometimes left us for half an hour now that we were older, there'd always been the two of us. I found myself tiptoeing nervously. It felt as if the house was waiting for me to do something.

"Don't be silly!" I told myself out loud, my voice echoing in the empty hall.

I grabbed a backpack and raided the kitchen for bread and cookies, a couple of apples, a chocolate bar, and a bottle of soda, which I stuffed in. The backpack was getting heavy. I realized I could change into jeans if I wanted to, now that I was home, so I did that, too, and put a sweater into the pack. I looked at my jacket where it hung from a peg by the front door, but it was a lovely, sunny morning in the middle of summer. I'd be home well before dark; no way did I need a coat.

I'd already worked out that everyone would get upset about my disappearing, of course. I'd been thinking that it would serve them right, especially Ruby, and Dad, too, for making me ride Thunder, but now I thought about police searches and stuff like that. A huge fuss wouldn't help me look clever or brave; just stupid and thoughtless. And it wouldn't be much good going off alone and getting hauled back in disgrace in the first five minutes, either. If only I had a cell phone; unfortunately, Dad had a thing about not letting us have one until we were thirteen. It's a little ironic, considering he was joined to his at the hip. Of course, if I told the others, I could probably borrow one of theirs. I wondered for a moment whether it would be better to creep back and tell them, but then I remembered I couldn't get into Hannah's house. More importantly, I wouldn't have minded telling Hannah or Abi, especially Abi, about my plans, but not Ruby. Not after the way she'd been last night.

I was losing time. Tanya would be up and taking care of the ponies soon. The only thing I could think of was to write notes. They'd all be lies, but hopefully that wouldn't get me into too much trouble.

I scribbled a note that said, "I decided to go back home to sleep. Sorry. Poppy x" and another saying, "Have taken Thunder out for an early ride – everyone knows. Ruby" and pushed them both into my pocket. Then I shot upstairs and drew the curtains in my room and squashed a spare comforter in a sausage shape under mine so it looked like I was asleep. I shut the door and then had a brilliant idea and wrote a third note – "Asleep. Please don't disturb" – and stuck that on the outside of my bedroom door. Not that anyone would be getting that far for a while – no one else had a key and Dad was playing golf miles away.

I hoisted the backpack onto my back, closed the front door behind me, and then ran as fast as I could back to Hannah's, where I pushed my first note under the door, so they'd find it when they got up. That wouldn't be for a long time, anyway – Hannah's family all liked to sleep in on Sundays, and we'd gotten to bed late. Then I sprinted along to the stables, and hung around by the entrance for a while to see if anyone was around.

Everything was absolutely still. I crept into the tack room and picked up Thunder's tack. The saddle was heavy and it was hard to keep the stirrups from chinking, especially as I was carrying the bridle, with its clanking bits of metal, in the other hand. The only way to be silent was to walk really slowly, which was so nerve-wracking. I expected to hear Tanya shouting from her window at any moment.

I deposited everything on the ground at the far corner of the yard, close to where the trail started, and went to get Thunder. The ponies were scattered around the paddock, some still asleep, others head down munching grass. Dandy was close the fence and I suddenly wondered whether I should take him instead. I'd been too busy getting ready and making plans to think about the actual riding up to now, but the butterflies that plagued me every time I had to ride Thunder had flooded back, and Dandy would be so much easier to manage. I nearly changed my mind and went back for his tack instead, but then I realized I'd be copping out yet again, and no one would have any more respect for me than before. It would have to be Thunder.

I'd need some sugar lumps and a head collar rope to catch him quickly and quietly. Back in the tack room, I reread the second note I'd written, the one that pretended to be from Ruby. I figured that Tanya would accept that as true and not worry for quite a while. Theoretically, we could go and ride our own pony whenever we liked, though she always kept an eye on what we were up to, and Ruby and Hannah had been out early several times that summer. I was hoping that Tanya would be so busy with her Sunday morning lessons that she wouldn't bother about Ruby going out on her own this time, or notice when she didn't come back soon, either.

I stuck the note on the peg where Thunder's bridle hangs and stood still for a moment, thinking through my plans and checking for anything I missed. I was seriously proud of myself for making so many complicated arrangements.

Whenever I'd read books about people running away, I'd always seen the holes in their plans, and thought how careless the author was. It just shows that reading's useful, I thought. My plan was foolproof; it was just for a couple of hours, probably, but that would be long enough for me to get well away from the village.

Before the really challenging part, riding Thunder (I was trying not to let myself think about that), there was still one more hard thing to do – catch him quietly and get him away from the stables before Tanya appeared. It was quarter to seven already; I was sure she'd get up early. Outdoorsy people always do.

I put three or four sugar lumps into a pocket for later, and clutched one in my hand. I climbed the paddock fence and walked toward Thunder as steadily as I could force myself. I wanted to hurry, but I knew that could lead to disaster if he got spooked, or decided to play games, or just cantered off around the paddock for some morning exercise. Dandy trotted up to me curiously and followed as I approached Thunder, which turned out to be very useful, because Thunder saw Dandy coming and came toward us to touch noses with him, which was so sweet and made me feel warmer toward Thunder than I'd ever felt before. I sidled around to his flank while he wasn't looking and clipped the rope onto his head collar by his mouth. He resisted being pulled away, obviously wanting a nice long early morning chat with Dandy, so I tugged a little harder and the rope fell onto the ground. Drat!

I didn't feel I could waste any more time reattaching it so I grabbed the nosepiece and offered him the sugar and he stepped after me. Dandy came along, too, and then we were joined by a couple of the riding school ponies, all inquisitive and friendly, and probably all hoping for a lump of sugar, too. That was all very well, but not exactly ideal for me if I wanted to make a quick getaway, as they were jostling around me and making harrumphing noises. The noise of their hoofs, even on the grass, might carry if they all took off at a gallop.

We got to the paddock gate. I struggled to open it one-handed while holding Thunder and at the same time fending off the rest of the ponies. The bolt was stiff and when it finally gave, the gate swung wide much faster than I'd intended. I turned toward Thunder to urge him through and, behind me, Socks came up and shouldered past me out into the open yard. His hoofs clattered noisily on the concrete. The other ponies were ready to follow him. Oh, no!

Chapter Eight

Panic rose in my throat. Frenziedly, I pulled Thunder through the gate and at the same time pushed it back against the mob of ponies that seemed to be following their herd instinct to all do the same thing. Thunder didn't like that. He stopped still and tensed his front legs and I had to tug wildly at him to get him to step forward again. The rest of the ponies clustered around the opening, luckily creating a bottleneck. I hissed "Back, back!" as fiercely as I could and that seemed to halt the flow enough for me to squeeze the gate shut against them, with Thunder and me on the right side.

Socks hadn't gone very far; he'd stopped just outside the gate and had put his head down into a stray tuft of grass that none of the ponies could reach from inside the paddock fence. I thought fast. I couldn't hold onto Thunder while I dealt with Socks, and if I let Thunder go, he might wander off on his own, too, and I couldn't tie him up, could

I? I'd just have to leave Socks where he was and pray he wouldn't move while I got Thunder bridled.

Thunder followed me obediently across the yard to where I'd left the tack, out of sight of Tanya's window, and I slid the bit into his mouth and the bridle over his head in record time. It's amazing what a little panic can do. As soon as I'd done up enough buckles to know the bridle wouldn't actually slip off, I wound the reins around a fence post and raced back to get Socks.

He wasn't there! For a long moment, I stood still and gazed around; how could he just disappear? Then I saw him. He'd wandered over to the stable block and was under the shadow of its eaves, right next to Roland's stall; in fact, as I watched, Roland's head appeared over the half door. He whinnied ear-piercingly loudly, as if to say hi to this unexpected visitor. Things were getting farcical.

I shot across the yard and fumbled a lump of sugar into my hand. I held it out to Roland who lipped it gently and started to crunch, which shut him up, and offered another to Socks. I grabbed his head collar to pull him back to the paddock while he was busy, whispering "Shhh!" to Roland as I went – not that he'd have understood or taken any notice, of course. The rest of the ponies were still bunched up by the gate. I opened it just enough to allow Socks through to join his friends. He walked back in perfectly happily, as if to say he'd enjoyed his excursion but would like to have breakfast now, thank you very much. His head went down to the grass instantly, and I closed the gate firmly with a giant sigh of relief.

So far, so good.

But then, I glanced up at the house and saw a hand pulling back curtains! I flew across the yard, around the corner, out of sight, panting and skidding to a stop next to Thunder. Had Tanya seen the shadow of movement as I shot out of sight? Had she heard suspicious noises or was she just getting up at her normal time? Did she draw the curtains back just before coming out to check everything, or was it the first thing she did, before showering and all that? Would she look out at the ponies and count them, and notice one was missing?

I waited, absolutely still, for an agonizing count of sixty seconds. Nothing happened. Then I dared stick my head around the corner to see if anything was going on. Still nothing. The curtains were open but I couldn't see any movement. I stole a glance toward to the paddock to see if there was anything out of the ordinary there. All the ponies had settled down again, and there were surely enough of them that she wouldn't notice one missing until later on, and then she'd see my note and think Ruby was out with Thunder, anyway. All I had to do was get Thunder saddled up and ride him out of the yard and down the trail, with as little noise and as quickly as was humanly possible.

I rejoined Thunder, who was looking rather puzzled at this change of routine. He watched me curiously as I lifted the saddle onto his back and did up the girth. The stirrups were going to be too long for me, but I didn't want to waste time adjusting them yet. I drew them down the leathers and gathered the reins in my right hand, ready to mount.

It was actually easier than usual because the stirrups were so long, since I didn't have to reach far, but once I was in the saddle it was like riding without stirrups. I wrapped my legs as close to Thunder's sides as I could and squeezed firmly, shaking the reins and chirruping encouragingly at the same time, and he stepped forward eagerly. Not letting the reins get any longer, I let him walk behind the stable block to where there was a narrow entrance to the trail. He brushed past the fence a little too close, squashing my leg, and I stifled a squeak of pain, but it wasn't intentional. I just hadn't directed him very well. A moment later we were out of the stables and walking along the trail.

And then I realized I'd forgotten my hard hat. I didn't have my back protector, either, but we didn't always have to wear those. I'd never, ever ridden without a hard hat, though. We kept them in the tack room, so now I'd have to go all the way back there to get it, or risk hurting myself really badly if I fell. That was all too likely if my record on Thunder was anything to go by.

I pulled Thunder to a halt and sat there wasting time arguing with myself. Hat or no hat? Risk getting caught or set off now, safe from detection? Then it struck me that my story relied on everything looking normal. Tanya would never accept that Ruby had gone out without her hat, so there it was, a no-brainer. I'd have to go back.

Thunder was getting restless by now. If someone was taking him out for a nice early ride, why couldn't she get on with it? I was still holding the reins very tightly because I could feel him trying to stretch his neck and I was frightened he'd shoot off before I was ready. So I dismounted very fast, slipping over his back, grabbing the noseband before he could register that I was off, and slung the reins around the gatepost again. I ran back into the stable yard, checked that everything was still quiet and then sprinted back to the tack room.

The hats had been piled up randomly yesterday after the party and it took me a while to disentangle mine from the others – and then I realized I'd have to take Ruby's or Tanya would definitely smell a rat. This was all getting so complicated! Ruby's dark green hat was a bit big for me, but I squashed my hair up into it to fill the space and did up the strap with trembling fingers, ready to run back to Thunder.

Halfway back across the yard, I heard the house door open ...

I tensed for a second, and then ran on. Perhaps Tanya wouldn't look my way. There were only a few yards to go.

"Hey, Ruby!"

I stopped in my tracks, but I didn't look around.

"Going out early again? You okay?"

I waved wildly as if I was really happy and yelled, "Yes, fine!" and kept going toward the stable block and onto the trail. I undid Thunder's reins and scrambled onto him, kicking his sides hard. He responded with an instant canter, down the familiar trail and away from the stables, and I clung on and went through what had happened over and over. So Tanya had seen me; hopefully she thought I was Ruby since my hair was all hidden in Ruby's hat. Then she'd go into the tack room and see the note and, with any luck, she wouldn't do any checking up or anything. As I said, we were entitled to take our own ponies out whenever we liked.

At any rate, it was too late now to worry. I'd done it, I'd taken Thunder out on my own, and now it was up to me to prove that I could ride him. It suddenly occurred to me that I hadn't had any trouble with him, not really. He'd been obedient and gentle and a perfect pony, despite being pushed around at the crack of dawn. Because I'd been focused on escaping, and not on riding, I hadn't been frightened, and he hadn't had any fear to pick up on from me. Maybe things wouldn't be so bad, after all.

He probably loved this fast canter, but the longer it went on the more I wasn't. I was bouncing and swaying from side to side, and every time Thunder stumbled as his foot hit an uneven bit of ground I expected to fall off. The stirrups were swinging freely since they were so long. One of them bashed my shin really hard and they must've been hurting Thunder, too. He probably thought they were telling him to go faster.

I stretched forward to try to grab the reins, which were flapping loosely, and felt the backpack swivel heavily on my back, taking me further off balance. Leaning forward seemed to be encouraging Thunder to go quicker, too. I sat back down in the saddle, grabbed the pommel, let myself bounce along uncomfortably for a few seconds, and then tried again. This time, I held on tight with one hand and gathered the reins with the other, which isn't as easy as it sounds, especially since Thunder's neck lengthened and pulled away at every stride. Still, I concentrated very hard and gradually, inch by inch, the reins shortened, and I was able to let go of the saddle and grab hold of a bunch of leather with my other hand, too.

"Ouch!" I screeched. Now that I wasn't holding on I'd bounced forward and landed on top of the pommel, and it really, really hurt. I was so far forward that my legs were more or less wrapped around Thunder's neck. I could feel the muscles beneath me stretching and relaxing. No way was I going to be able to stay on ...

I hit the ground with a thump and winded myself. I lay there, rolled up in a ball, gasping for breath and panting for what seemed like forever. Once things relaxed and I could breathe normally again, I sat up slowly, wondering if I'd injured myself. My back felt strange until I realized the backpack was digging into me. No bones seemed to be broken; I flexed my arms and legs and nothing hurt specifically, though I felt a little sore all over. So I stood up, a little gingerly, and brushed myself off, and felt infinitely grateful that I'd decided to go back for the hard hat, even if it was a little big and had skewed sideways over one eye.

Then I remembered I was responsible for Thunder, even if I didn't want to be. Amazingly, he hadn't disappeared into the distance. Instead, he was standing quite still at the edge of the trail. He was an awful mess. His saddle must have twisted as I fell off and was dangling from one side. One stirrup was dragging on the ground and the other was tangled up with his mane. The reins were trailing, too, and because I hadn't done up the bridle properly, the throat lash was hanging loose. He eyed me suspiciously, as if to blame me for what had happened.

I looked back at him and thought for a while. It hadn't been the greatest start to our day, but we were both okay, and it actually had been a sort of adventure, hadn't it? Stealing out of the house, sneaking off with Thunder, and racing away from Tanya all started to seem quite exciting and even glamorous. I pictured myself telling Ruby and the other two about how we'd galloped down the trail. I found myself wondering if maybe I shouldn't go home now and tell them all about it, and then that would be that.

I pushed my hat back into place and wriggled the backpack into a comfier position. Holding my hand out flat so that he'd think I was offering him something nice, I approached Thunder. He stepped back, shaking his head,

97

looking spooked. I took another careful step forward and he shivered all over, as if I'd really scared him.

"Here, boy, sugar," I said, digging in my jeans pocket for the last, crumbly lump and holding it out. I didn't get any nearer, but just waited to let him decide. I could see him wondering if it was wise to come back to me. Perhaps it would show more intelligence if he didn't trust me. I hadn't exactly treated him well yet, had I?

I wiggled my hand around to draw his attention to the sugar but he just rolled his eyes dramatically, showing the whites oddly, and took a sharp step backwards. I could see his muscles tightening. Was he about to fly off down the trail? And if so, which way – toward the safety of his stable, or out into the wide blue yonder, where it would be my fault if he got lost, or injured, or even killed?

I shuffled around to position myself between him and the way to the river. If it came to it, I'd prefer him to turn for home; the alternative was too scary to contemplate.

I couldn't bear to wait any longer.

"Sugar, nice sugar," I whispered in the gentlest voice I could manage and took a tentative step closer. For a long tense moment he stared down at my hand while I kept up a murmur of comforting sounds, and then he extended his neck and nosed the sugar from as far away as he could. Finally, he opened his big mouth and crunched it down, and at long last I was able to get hold of the reins.

"Poor old Thunder," I crooned, stroking his neck rhythmically. "Let's get you straightened out now, nice and gently."

Trying to move slowly and not alarm him any more, I fixed the bridle and made sure the bit was properly in his mouth. He breathed heavily onto my hand, dribbling

98

sticky bits of sugar, and I stroked the soft skin around his nose, and traced the long white blaze up between his ears. It was the most affectionate moment I'd ever had with Thunder.

A while later, I pulled the reins back over his head and kept hold of them as I straightened out the saddle. The girth needed tightening and he stood calmly as I swapped sides, watching me curiously.

"Okay, Thunder?"

He snorted as if in reply.

This time, I shortened the stirrups to what seemed a better length and came around to his front to have another stroking session before mounting. Despite trying to be confident, I was starting to get nervous again. Maybe I *should* call it a day at this stage?

If I did, would I feel any better about riding Thunder in the future? After all, all I'd done so far was ride him out of control and fall off. How was that going to help me? No, I'd have to get back on and keep going, until I could hold my head up high and feel certain that I actually could ride my own pony. And after that, I'd be able to reclaim some respect and trust from Ruby, Dad, and the others.

With a heavy heart, I got hold of the reins and the pommel with my left hand, reached my foot up to the stirrup, and hauled myself into the saddle. Thunder fidgeted restlessly as I got myself settled and I tried as I had before to keep the reins tight. At least this time my feet were firmly in the stirrups. I touched his sides with my heels and pulled my right hand sideways to guide him further down the trail. We wouldn't be going home, not yet.

I held Thunder back to a slow walk, pacing steadily along the rough trail, and gradually I relaxed and started to enjoy myself a little bit. The sun had risen higher and was warm on my front, and the woods on either side of the trail looked so beautiful, with dappled light on wildflowers, tall trees and rough grass. It was eight o'clock now. No one had come searching for us, so Tanya must have believed it was Ruby that she'd seen, and Hannah's household was guaranteed to still be fast asleep.

Whenever we rode down the trail alone, we weren't allowed over the bridge but, of course, this time I was going to have to cross it. The alternative would be to turn around and go straight back to the stables. My vague plan was to start by following the route I'd traveled with the group a couple of weeks before, which had taken about two hours, but instead to continue in a much bigger loop across the wild open plains that bordered the woodland I was traveling through at the moment. I didn't have a map, but I did have a picture in my head of the route I'd need to take, as we'd been onto the plains with Dad in the car quite a lot for walks and picnics. There was a whole network of lanes that crisscrossed the area with lots of signposts, too. Also, I knew that if I followed the sun, I'd be going east at first and later south, so, later in the day, all I'd have to do would be to go west, toward the sun as it set, and I should get back to where I started. It all seemed perfectly logical.

Unfortunately, though, none of my plans would work if I couldn't get Thunder over the river, and he took one look at that rickety bridge and dug his heels in. No way was he going over that!

Chapter Nine

This was going to be a challenge, but it wasn't really so much about my being frightened of riding Thunder. It was more about my giving him enough confidence that nothing awful would happen if he stepped onto those planks. I dismounted and tried walking alongside Thunder, clicking my tongue encouragingly, but it didn't work. He was a lot stronger than I, so when he said no, I couldn't pull him. And I certainly didn't have any authority over him; he didn't particularly trust me, so he didn't feel any reason to do as I asked if his instincts went against me.

I led him around in a half-circle so we were facing back down the trail and stood by him quietly, stroking his neck. He seemed all right then, but when I turned him back toward the bridge he reacted in exactly the same way, leaning back onto his hind legs away from it, his front legs firmly planted in the ground.

"Come *on*, Thunder!" I yelled at him angrily, in the hope

that shouting would make a difference, but I was wasting my breath. I went through the turning away and stroking routine again and had another brainstorm.

Years ago, I'd read a pony story where there was a fire in a stable and the heroine had to get the terrified horses out safely. She'd done it by putting blankets over their heads so that they couldn't see the flames, and then they'd followed quite easily. Would something like that work for Thunder? If he couldn't see the bridge, might he forget it existed?

It had to be worth a try. After all, the only alternative was to go home, humiliated.

I didn't have a blanket, but there was the sweater I'd stuffed into the backpack. I fished it out and looked at it doubtfully. It didn't look big enough to cover Thunder's face, but then it was only his eyes that needed to be blindfolded. I reached up a little nervously and draped it over his ears so that it hung down over his blaze. He reacted by shaking his head, and the sweater fell off. He nosed it on the ground in a puzzled sort of way, as if he was wondering how it got there, but he didn't seem especially scared by it, so I tried again.

This time I tucked the arms under the headband and let the main part of the sweater fall gently over Thunder's eyes. He shook his head again, but this time it stayed in place. His ears twitched and he shook his head again. While all that was happening, I pulled on the reins and he followed me, as if he wasn't thinking about anything but this strange darkness that had suddenly descended onto him. Holding my breath, I led him firmly onto the bridge. His hoofs echoed dramatically and he slowed down.

"Come on, boy," I said as matter-of-factly as I could manage.

102

To my utter relief, this time he kept going. He walked peacefully across as if he'd never made a fuss before. On the other side, I pulled off the blindfold and told him how clever he was, and he pushed his head into my chest the way Dandy used to. He let me caress his ears, and I started to believe for the first time that this was my pony, and not just some alien creature imposed upon me by Dad.

I had to remount, and even feeling better about Thunder didn't change the fact that he was a long way up. He set off before I was properly in the saddle, with me flailing around wildly trying to get my right leg in place. I dropped the reins, too. The only good thing was that I knew this time he'd only go in one direction – onwards.

Once I had myself straightened out, I walked him for a long time and actually started to find that kind of boring. So I pressed his sides with my heels and leaned forward a little bit, and we went into a nice smooth trot, just like the last time I'd ridden down this trail, with Hannah and all the others. After all the excitement of the initial race and then getting over the bridge, he'd lost the first flush of enthusiasm and seemed content to go along at a reasonable pace without pulling to go into a canter. This was actually fun!

Eventually, we reached a gate from the trail, which led onto open grassland. I knew the way we usually went was over to the right, following the line of the woods we'd just come through, and back into them again as far as the main road, but my plan was to strike out in a different direction, or else I'd be back much too soon to make my point. Anyway, I wasn't in any hurry to get back at the moment. I was finally enjoying myself.

On the other hand, I was absolutely starving. I hadn't

had anything to eat for breakfast and the morning was coming to an end.

At least if I stopped here, there'd be a gate to tie Thunder to. Once we were on the plains, trees would be few and far between. So I dismounted and hooked the reins over the gate. Thunder put his head down instantly toward the scrubby grass at his feet. We'd always been told not to let our ponies graze when they were bridled, but I was worried that if I took Thunder's bridle off he'd head out and leave me stranded, so I decided to ignore the rules and let him enjoy his snack. It probably wasn't any more important than all the other silly rules we got told by grownups all the time. I loosened the girth and ran the stirrups up the leathers and left him to his meal.

The bread I'd brought turned out to be stale and hard to eat without honey or butter or anything, so I scattered it for the birds to break their beaks on and ate the chocolate instead. It was already getting soft, so I reasoned there was no point in leaving any of it to get really squidgy and horrible as the day got hotter. Then I swigged back some soda, and finished with one of my apples. I shared the core with Thunder, and he crunched and dribbled happily.

It was the nicest breakfast, sitting there comfortably with my back against the gate, looking out over the gorgeous wild plains, with a peaceful, obedient pony nibbling the grass next to me. In fact it was so comfortable, and so warm, that I dozed off.

Luckily, an airplane flew over, quite low, and I woke up with a start. I checked my watch; I'd been asleep for nearly half an hour.

I couldn't allow myself to sleep here. We were still on the main trail used by the riding school, which was the first place they'd search for me. And even if they weren't looking for me, there was likely to be a trail ride going out that morning. I'd look really silly if they tripped over me. So I packed everything away, including the chocolate wrapper, to hide that I'd been there and also to keep from polluting the countryside, of course, and got Thunder ready for another ride.

"It's all a little stop-and-go today, isn't it, boy?" I said to him as I ran the stirrups down the leathers and checked the girth. "You must be wondering what on earth we're doing. Well, now we're going to have a nice ride over the plains, nice and slowly, okay?"

I felt kind of like an idiot talking to Thunder like that, and yet I'd always talked to Dandy, who seemed to understand more or less what I was saying. I'd never really tried talking to Thunder before today, because apart from not especially wanting to, I'd assumed he didn't much like me. But now his ears pricked intelligently when he heard my voice, and he waited patiently as I scrambled onto his back; for once he didn't start off until I was ready and gave him the signal. Things were definitely looking up.

Ahead of us, the plains rose steeply toward the far off blue horizon. I was pretty sure we'd meet a road that crossed at right angles if we kept going for long enough. I remembered a particular picnic we'd had one afternoon when Dad had been trying to show us how to read a map, where there was a parking lot right on the plains, surrounded by dramatic outcrops of rock which Ruby and I had scrambled over. It'd be nice to spend some time exploring there, and all I'd have to do afterwards would be to retrace my footsteps, or rather Thunder's hoof steps, back to where we were now. Then I could either go back over the bridge and risk Thunder refusing, or I could go the longer way home, via the main road. Either way, I couldn't possibly get lost.

I felt a warm glow inside as I imagined how impressed everyone would be when I rode confidently into the stable yard in the afternoon.

Thunder took his time going uphill. I left the reins long and allowed him to pick his own path through and around the tufts of grass and stunted bushes. Sometimes he stumbled, but at that speed my balance was fine. I was preoccupied with thinking about Ruby and how the two of us had drifted apart and why. I remembered how enthusiastically she'd welcomed my suggestion of moving into different bedrooms, and relived the hurt I'd felt at the time. I went over and over the horrible arguments of the last couple of days and all the barbed remarks she'd made. All that made me feel really upset again and a few tears rolled down my face.

Thunder jogged along quietly as I wallowed in misery. When I looked up, I realized just how lonely the countryside had become. There were no signs of human life anywhere; just open grassland, a few trees and bushes, and rocks. There was nothing I recognized, either. I'd expected to see Dad's parking lot pretty much right away. I pulled Thunder to a stop and swiveled in the saddle to look back the way I'd come. The woods were still visible in the distance, and beyond them I could just make out what might be the glint of sunlight on roofs; that must be our village, miles and miles away.

"Pull yourself together, Poppy," I said out loud to myself. "You're not lost and you know what you're doing."

And stop rambling on about the past, I added silently.

After all, I couldn't change what had already happened, could I? What I had to do was to sort out the future.

Thunder whinnied suddenly, bringing me sharply back to the present. He was gazing, head held high, to the right. I looked too, and saw the most amazingly beautiful sight; a herd of deer was running parallel to us, their golden coats shining in the sun. Some of them had fantastic curling antlers, and to complete the picture, there were some sweet Bambi-like babies, working doubly hard to keep up with their mothers, leaping and jumping for fun. Thunder whinnied again and broke straight into a canter, following the herd. I grabbed the reins, sat as firmly as I could in the saddle, and tried to keep him from galloping. I felt I could just about cope with a canter but I didn't need another fall; I was already sore enough.

For once I completely understood why Thunder wanted to chase after the deer and I didn't have the heart to stop him, assuming I could have, of course.

The deer must have been frightened by us because they sped up sharply. I struggled to keep Thunder under control, especially as we were now going well off my planned route. My riding must have been improving. I'm sure a day or two before I'd have fallen off, but this time I stayed on and moved with my pony rather than against him, actually enjoying the sensation of whizzing along. We were galloping now despite my efforts, but it was all right. My feet were still in the stirrups and the fresh air against my face and the wind on my arms were exhilarating. Thunder thundered along, his mane flying alongside my hands and his strong body focused on speed. I gripped tighter with my legs as he stumbled momentarily, but he regained his balance and shot on. I'd given up all attempts at slowing him down and was just allowing myself to enjoy the sensation of speed and being at one with my pony. It was all so cool.

Thunder eventually slackened his crazy pace and let the herd go on without us. They were just too fast. He slowed gradually, and I was able to gather the reins more closely in my hands, sit up straighter and almost pretend to myself that I had something to do with the process. Not that I really cared. I'd finally discovered why Ruby and Hannah loved going so fast, and I felt a mixture of wild pride that I'd done it, and shame that I'd been such a wuss before.

"Okay, whoa now," I sang out to Thunder, guiding him into a circle that finally controlled him and then drawing him to a halt. I leaned forward and patted his shining, sweaty neck. "Such a good boy," I murmured, my hair mixing with his mane. "Wasn't that the best ride ever?"

He snorted as if in agreement and stood still, his chest heaving as he got his breath back. It occurred to me that he might get a chill if he stood around and also that he must be thirsty on such a hot day. The only water we'd passed so far had been the river by the dreaded bridge.

I stood up in the stirrups to get my bearings. I didn't recognize where I was, but the sun was still blazing down and I reckoned I'd gone far enough from home. That meant I should be turning south, which meant going toward the sun, since it was almost noon. There seemed to be a valley ahead, and valleys have streams, don't they? I nudged my heels against Thunder's sides and steered him slightly right, and he obeyed without a fuss, walking slowly, still breathing heavily. As we went along, I kept up a rhythmic stroking of his neck, and hummed a song contentedly, and he responded by flicking his ears as if he was enjoying it.

I suddenly felt so happy and confident about riding. If I could keep on doing what I'd just done, then I never needed to worry about riding ever again. I'd proved myself. In fact, I might just as well start back for home, before anyone got too panicky about my being missing, and then I'd be able to talk to Ruby on an equal level for the first time in ages. For the first time, I thought that maybe she hadn't been entirely unfair to me. Maybe I was the one who had been a pain, continually moaning about Thunder and refusing to try to ride him properly. Maybe I'd been hankering after Dandy in a really babyish way. Could it be that the reason she'd been glad to move rooms was because I wasn't all that nice to share with any longer?

It's not much fun discovering that you haven't been as right as you think you have. I always knew I was being a little cowardly, of course, but I'd always been able to justify my feelings and blame other people for being unkind, or over-competitive, or whatever. All my certainties about my behavior suddenly drained away, but this time I wasn't going to feel sorry for myself and burst into tears. This time I'd become a stronger person, and I was determined not to be a coward ever again.

As we went slightly downhill, we seemed to be following a narrowing route between sharp rocks, and when we finally reached the edge of the valley Thunder stopped suddenly, alarmed. I peered forward over his shoulder and saw a steep rocky hillside stretching down in front of us. It looked far too dangerous for Thunder to get down, but I couldn't see any other route, unless we went back the way we'd come. I clicked my tongue and encouraged him to go forward. He hesitated, so I kicked gently and he took a reluctant step forward. His hoof

109

skidded out from under him immediately and he only just recovered himself; for a second I could picture the pair of us tumbling downhill, legs flailing. I swung him away from the slope quickly. Should I set him walking along the top, waiting for it to get shallower? I could see the gleam of the waterway down below and it made me so thirsty; I swigged the last few mouthfuls of soda and felt guilty that I couldn't share it with Thunder.

I'd been riding toward the sun but it was so high in the sky now that it was hard to tell which way was south. It seemed to me that the line of the valley led vaguely in the direction of home, so, as it seemed extremely unlikely I'd ever find Dad's parking lot now, I decided we'd pick our way along the top of the valley and see where it got us.

I was becoming more and more aware of how worried they must be at home by now. Would Dad know yet? I hated the idea of making him worried. Would they be sending out search parties? There was still no sign of anyone around; the last human trace I'd seen was the glimpse of the village, miles ago. On the other hand, whenever we'd been out on the plains before, there had seemed to be lots of crisscrossing roads. Thinking logically, I surmised that soon I would come across either a road or the woods leading back to the village, or something that would give me some indication of where I was.

If I didn't, I would have to accept that I might have achieved my goal of learning to enjoy riding and being independent and brave, but that I was also totally lost in the middle of an enormous wilderness area.

Chapter Ten

It turned out to be impossible to ride Thunder along the edge of what was rapidly becoming a steep gorge. There was only a narrow gap between the precipice on our left and the hill on our right, which was a mixture of rough rock and scrubby, spiky trees. I slid off carefully and passed the reins over his head. There was just enough space for me, ducking and twisting, to lead him. He followed reluctantly but obediently, head down, picking a safe route for himself but still stumbling now and again.

A long time later, the ledge widened out very briefly and I stopped to catch my breath and to think. Looking back made me gasp in horror. How on earth had we gotten this far without an accident? And looking forward wasn't much better. I hated what I was doing, and what I was making my pony do. We were in genuine danger on this wobbly ledge, and if one of us got hurt it would all be my fault. But there was no alternative. We couldn't turn back, because there just wasn't enough room for a pony to turn around, even at this wider point. We were trapped in a nightmare situation.

If I'd been alone, I think I'd have panicked and frozen. In fact, I'd probably still be there, waiting to be rescued. But I had to keep going, for my pony's sake. He hadn't done anything wrong today, apart from not wanting to cross the bridge, and I could understand his being scared of that. He'd had enormous fun chasing after the deer, but a good rider could have stopped him at any moment, and the rest of the time he'd been well behaved and good-natured, even when I was asking him to do ridiculous things like teetering along the edge of a precipice, which no sensible pony would choose to do.

No, it was all my responsibility, so I couldn't allow us to get stuck. And we needed to get to water. My mouth was dry and I found myself licking my lips constantly, and Thunder must have been desperate for a drink after hours and hours in this heat without a drink.

I pulled on the reins, clicked my tongue encouragingly, and Thunder started after me. The ground sloped steeply to the side now and was rough and stony. Several times I skidded and had to save myself, heart thumping wildly, from disappearing downhill. Thunder was actually better at negotiating the hillside than I was; maybe because he had four legs, he was much more sure-footed. There was one terrifying moment when he was on the brink of almost sliding away, but he scrabbled wildly and regained his footing, snorting and whinnying. My arm holding the reins behind me was trembling with tension and my legs with tiredness, but I couldn't risk stopping while the way was so dangerous. I might be balanced properly at any particular moment, but Thunder might not be.

After what seemed like hours, we were going uphill, not because I wanted to but because it was the only way I could see to go, and ahead there was a pointed rock and the narrowest of spaces between it and the hillside, It looked really risky. I had no idea what might be on the other side; maybe a sheer drop? All I could see beyond was blue sky.

I halted for a moment, considering my options. There'd still been no safe places to turn Thunder, and if I lost the momentum of the journey, I was scared he'd panic and then we really would be in trouble. While I kept going steadily, he seemed to believe that I knew what I was doing and that he'd be safe. I took a deep breath and clambered up, dragging Thunder, who was understandably reluctant to scrabble up this steep, slippery slope. We finally reached the top and I stopped dead, petrified that I'd fall straight down.

I'd have shouted with relief if I hadn't been afraid that it would frighten Thunder. There wasn't a precipice. At long last, the ledge was widening in front of us into what looked like a proper path, and best of all, it was winding downwards, toward the bottom of the valley, where there had to be a stream.

Thunder nuzzled my shoulder and harrumphed as if he too recognized that the worst of this trek was over. I stroked his long nose and felt his soft muzzle and the warm breath in the palm of my hand.

"Time to get moving," I said, sliding the reins back over his head and mounting as quickly as my exhausted legs would allow. "They'll be getting panicked if we don't get home soon. Go on, boy."

Thunder snorted as if he understood, and we set off downhill. I couldn't let him go very fast, because it was still steep and slippery, but compared to that snail-like crawling along the ledge, we were motoring along. The countryside was different on this side of the hill. We'd left the open plains behind, and soon we were in deep forest, with tall fir trees looming up all around us. It was pretty dark, though I could see glimpses of the blue sky way up high between the branches, and cooler than before, which was a relief, but spookily quiet. Apart from the echoing clatter of Thunder's hoofs, which gradually became muffled by dead leaves as we went further down the path, there didn't seem to be any birds, or animals, or anything.

The silence started to get to me after a while. I found I was shivering even though it wasn't cold, and I was sitting much too stiffly in the saddle. The back of my neck was tense and tight and I jerked at the reins by mistake when Thunder stumbled momentarily on a hidden stone.

I pulled him to a standstill and patted him softly.

"Sorry, Thunder, did that hurt your mouth?"

He tossed his head.

"Okay. Let's keep on. Not long to the water now."

I was wrong. The path took forever, meandering between the trees. In fact, I'm not sure it was a path, because sometimes it seemed to fade away completely and then we'd wander around, see what looked like another opening and follow that. The only constant was that we were gradually going downhill, but I'd lost all faith that it might lead to water. This could be a slope for miles and miles and miles, for all I could tell. I was trying to guide Thunder to safety and I had absolutely no idea where safety might be.

To add to our problems, there was not only no water, but no grass either. The trees were too thickly grown, so the only vegetation was dead and would be useless for Thunder. I was desperate to stop and rest, but how could I when he wouldn't be able to eat or drink? Horses aren't like people, able to eat once or twice a day. They need regular chances to graze and drink ...

I was avoiding looking at my watch because it made me feel more stressed every time I realized how late it was getting. The possibility that I might have to spend the night out with Thunder in the middle of nowhere loomed over me. My stomach rumbled with hunger and eventually I decided to stop anyway, for a rest, and a chance to think clearly without worrying all the time if Thunder was going to skid.

The moment I got off, he put his head down at once and nosed around in the leaves, looking for something to nibble. All I had left in the backpack was the second apple and a packet of cookies. I looked longingly at that apple, my mouth salivating at the thought of its crisp juiciness, but Thunder's need was greater than mine. I held it out to him, and he snatched it off my hand and crunched it with real relish. Meanwhile, I struggled through some cookies. I'd never realized before how dry cookies are. Then I thought, cookies are made of oats and stuff, aren't they? So I offered Thunder one and he liked it, and we shared the rest.

I was still hanging onto the reins every time I got off just in case Thunder decided to bolt, but I really had to go to the bathroom now, so I hitched them over a branch, told him to be good, and went a few yards away. When I got back, he was standing patiently watching me, and as soon as I got near enough he thrust his head into my chest and snuffled lovingly.

"Dear, darling Thunder," I murmured, "I'm so sorry I

got us into this mess, but we'll be all right. Someone will find us, don't worry."

He lifted his head and looked at me, and snorted again, so that a fine spray of cookie crumbs splattered around me. That made me laugh. I stroked his forelock firmly and ran my hand down his white blaze to his velvety mouth, and realized I wasn't alone on my adventure. There were two of us, together.

The journey went on, and on, and on. You can't imagine how big that forest was, and I'd just about given up hope of ever seeing anything but trees ever again when there was a break ahead; a sliver of light instead of dark trunks, that widened and lightened. Thunder broke into a trot as we finally came to the edge of the forest.

I pulled Thunder to a stop and we looked out from the shelter of the trees into blinding sunlight. The sun was really low, and we were looking straight into it. For a moment, I was dazzled and I had to release the reins and rub my eyes. What I was hoping for was civilization; preferably a familiar village or, if not, something to do with people, or, at the very least, a stream.

It could have been a lot worse. We'd come out by a road. It was empty, stretching away into the distance in both directions, but it was a road, and roads have to go somewhere eventually. The only question was, which way should we go to get home fastest?

Although my plan to follow the sun didn't seem to be working very well, it was the only one I had. The road went north to south, assuming the sun was setting in the west, so logically north would be the better way. With luck, I'd soon get to a farm or house, and then they'd tell me where to go, or call home for me, or something. I kept visualizing Dad and Ruby looking for me, desperate for a call. If only I'd gotten hold of a cell phone!

I steered Thunder to the right and we started along the narrow road. No cars went by, no houses appeared. It seemed to be going from nowhere to nowhere. The trees thinned out on our right and we were surrounded by grassland again, undulating grassy tussocks and the same thorny bushes we'd seen all day. I was sick of them.

Gradually, though, the ground next to the road was getting softer and suddenly I could hear tinkling water. I didn't need to urge Thunder into a trot; he must have smelled the water, because, even though he must have been tired out, he sped up, headed off the road and found the spring all by himself. It was a miniature waterfall coming out between some rocks that trickled over a few yards of soggy ground before disappearing. I leaped off his back, knelt by the spring, and stuck my mouth under it so that the delicious cold liquid could fill me up. It was unbelievably blissful. Meanwhile, Thunder was next to me, his head down in the little stream, drinking and drinking and drinking. He lifted his head for a second, dripping water from his muzzle, blew contentedly, and drank some more.

We stayed there for a long time because I couldn't bring myself to leave the water. I'd kept the soda bottle so I filled it up, but that wasn't going to last very long. I kept looking at Thunder as he stood in the puddle of water and took occasional sips now that his thirst was sated, and worried about what would happen if we didn't find anywhere better.

Home felt like another world; the party yesterday and the big fight last night and then creeping off this morning all seemed impossibly distant. Of course I knew, logically, that they'd be searching for me. Which meant that if I stayed where I was there'd be a good chance someone would come along, and we'd be safe.

On the other hand, I hadn't set out on this trip with the idea that I'd need rescuing. My whole aim had been to prove myself, and getting lost wasn't exactly a part of that.

Another problem was that it was getting a little cold. The sun had set and the long summer evening was cool and breezy. I dug out my sweater and put it on, and felt a little better. I was starving, too. Apples, some chocolate, a few cookies and some dry bread that I'd stupidly thrown away – not a lot for a whole day outdoors. I reminded myself that I'd eaten so much yesterday that I wasn't very likely to come to any harm if I had a diet day today – in fact, I could pretend it was cleansing, as Hannah's mother did sometimes.

Pretending didn't actually make me feel less hungry, though, so eventually I decided we'd move on. We'd follow the road and that way we'd have to come to a house in the end. Poor Thunder didn't look exactly thrilled to see me gathering up the reins one more time, and reaching up to the stirrup nearly defeated me, I was so tired. In the end, I cheated by lengthening the leather on the left side and then shortening it once I'd hauled myself into the saddle.

"Okay, just one last stretch," I said cheerfully to Thunder, shaking the reins and adding, silently, "I hope."

We lumbered off down the empty, echoing road. It was still light out on the plains, but so lonely. We passed one or two more streams, so I felt reassured that we wouldn't run short of water again, and every now and again Thunder would pull away from the reins and lower his head to snatch a mouthful of grass.

118

"I know, I'm mean not letting you stop for more," I told him, hauling his head up for the twentieth time and kicking him on gently, "but I promise you'll have all you want when we get back."

Suddenly, there was something, way ahead. A blur of color that wasn't the continuous gray-green of the plains or gray-blue of the sky. A whirring, harsh noise, too. Something mechanical – engines? I pushed Thunder on quickly, in case whoever it was moved off before we reached them. Gradually, the blur emerged through the gathering dusk as a group of motorcycles all parked together, and a bunch of people dressed in leather and wearing helmets standing around, swigging from cans by the look of it. Their backs were to us. No one had seen us yet.

I slowed Thunder down, feeling nervous. Dad had told Ruby and me some real scary stories about motorcycle gangs and I'd read some nasty things, too. But on the other hand, they were people and they'd see I needed help, and I firmly believe that most people are kind and nice.

But we didn't get close enough to test out my theory. Just as we were getting near, there was a loud cheer and a burst of raucous laughter, and then the noise of bikes revving up. Thunder's ears went back and I could feel the terror shooting through his body. A split second later, three motorcycles roared past us at top speed, their engines pumping out fierce noise, the smell of hot metal and gasoline filling the air.

Thunder turned tail and bolted.

I should have been getting good at this. It wasn't the first time that day I'd been clinging on desperately, clutching at anything to stay on board, but this time was different. The first fast ride had been Thunder enjoying himself when he

119

was fresh and I was disorganized and pathetic. The second time, when he galloped after the deer, had been glorious even when I'd been a little scared. This time, though, he was absolutely terrified and so was I.

He veered away from the bikes instinctively and was immediately off the tarmac, the sharp clip-clopping I'd been enjoying for the last hour replaced by a frantic thumping of hoofs on grass and stone. I vaguely heard shouting behind me, and even the sound of a bike for a while, as if someone was following, but Thunder was crossing the roughest of ground and no normal motorcycle could have managed it. I had no chance of looking back to see what was happening anyway. I couldn't even really watch where we were going, as I was totally focused on staying on Thunder's back. My head was buried somewhere against his neck with my eyes shut half the time. But what I did see was glimpses of the same sort of rocky, horribly uneven ground that we'd been seeing all day, and then trees again. It was getting darker and gloomier by the second, and Thunder was swerving between the tree trunks and stumbling over bumpy hillocks and flying down slippery slopes.

Somehow, goodness knows how, my feet were still in the stirrups but I'd lost the reins and was hanging onto his neck, my arms almost meeting at the front. I tried to tighten them to make him gasp and choke and stop but I couldn't squeeze hard enough, and even in this situation I didn't want to hurt him.

At long last Thunder's wild pace slowed a little. The forest had gotten thicker and he couldn't maintain such a crazy gallop. I dared to sit up a little and felt around for the reins. The left side was hanging almost straight down from his bit. I leaned forward as much as I dared, feeling the pressure of my right foot against the stirrup iron as it splayed out sideways to counterbalance my weight. There was a terrifying split second when it felt as if I'd leaned too far and was going to catapult off. Then I lunged forward and grabbed the flying leather strap as it flapped back toward me, and managed to get my fingers around it enough to pull it back toward me.

The end was snapped off, so I could only connect to Thunder's mouth on one side, but that didn't keep me from tugging, pulling his head around. Instinctively, I felt that doing that would slow him down, and yes, it did. Gradually, he calmed down to a ragged canter and then to a jerky trot and almost instantly after, he stopped and stood still, head down, sweating and trembling.

Silence swept around us, muffled and eerie.

I was shaking, too. I slid off, murmuring little comforting things to cool Thunder down, and looked at the damage.

The reins hung loosely, torn apart. Bits of grass and dirt spattered Thunder's coat, which had been so glossy when we set out, and it was streaked with sweat. His mouth was foamy around the bit, and his nostrils flared as he took great breaths of air. His ears, which had been laid almost flat against his skull, were going back to their normal position, but his eyes still looked wild; he was rolling them dramatically at me, so that the whites glittered through the dusk.

Worst of all, on his right foreleg, there was a ragged tear, and blood was dripping down onto the dry ground.

Now what was I going to do?

Chapter Eleven

It would be dishonest not to admit that I burst into tears. I think anyone would have. It was such an awful situation. Not only had we gotten lost again, after finally finding a road, but it was now truly dark, we were hungry and thirsty, and, on top of that, I had an injured pony to deal with.

I say truly dark, but actually it wasn't quite that bad. The trees grew close together, but there were a few more open patches and there was still some late daylight, and maybe the moon would come out, as it had the night before. Was it really only last night when I'd been crouching by Hannah's window, planning my day's adventure?

I led Thunder into one of the clearings and squatted down to examine his leg. He was mouthing at it, and I had to push his head away to get a good look myself. It wasn't great. The flap of torn skin was the size of my finger, and hung down gruesomely, and behind and above it there was redness and dirt and oozing blood.

Thunder whimpered as I put my hand gently onto the wound, and stepped back sharply, making me lose my balance. I landed flat on my face in the soft messy leaf mold that covered the forest floor, and picked myself up slowly. Thunder had backed well away and was watching me warily, the two lengths of torn rein swinging slightly on either side of his head.

"Okay, boy, let me get hold of you and I'll fix you up," I murmured, approaching him cautiously. He tossed his head and took another step back, and another. Much more of this, and he'd merge into the dark trees where I'd lose him. Only his white blaze gleamed clearly now, along with the whites of his eyes that still showed his fear of what had happened to him.

I kept on speaking softly and soothingly, not making much sense, but I stayed exactly where I was, and thankfully, so did he.

Minutes passed as I stood there, watching him watch me. Bit by bit, his panicky breathing slowed, and for that matter so did mine. Still, behind the comforting muttering my mind was racing. I needed to get hold of Thunder, first to fix up his leg, and second, to make sure I didn't lose him. Then, I was going to have to camp here for the rest of the night, with the same old problem of no food or water, and that could mean keeping Thunder tied up. And finally, he'd been sweating buckets, which not only must have meant he was dreadfully thirsty but also that he might catch a chill if I didn't rub him down.

If only I'd taken more sugar, and not wasted it on all the other ponies! I carefully lowered my hand and felt about in my pocket, just in case I'd missed a little, but of course there wasn't any left.

Standing there looking at Thunder reminded me of those games when you stare each other down. Would it be better to maintain my stare or let my gaze drop? Maybe he'd prefer that?

Anyway, I had to blink eventually, as you always do, and at the same time I let myself sink cross-legged to the ground. I sat there very still, and just waited.

It seemed like a long time, in fact I'd sunk into a half doze, when I felt warm breath on my face. Thunder had come back to me, all by himself!

I grabbed a trailing rein with one hand and stayed there on the ground, letting him feel safe and secure, stroking any parts of him that I could reach. I could just make out his leg, and it looked like the bleeding had stopped. I wasn't going to try to do anything about it now, not if he wasn't bleeding to death or anything. After a while, I stood up, still patting him reassuringly, and felt his back. It was still damp with sweat. I twisted the longer end of rein around my wrist and slipped off the backpack, my sweater, and the T-shirt that I'd been wearing all day. Then I put the sweater back on again over bare skin so I'd be able to use the T-shirt to rub Thunder down.

First of all, though, I needed to untack him. He hadn't had his tack off all day and it must have been such a relief to finally get rid of the heavy saddle on his back. I dumped it on the ground but kept his bridle on for now. The longer rein was still too short to tie him up, so I tried to keep hold of it, but in the end it was just too difficult and I decided to let it go. After all, Thunder had had plenty of chances to leave me and he hadn't, so why would he now that I was finally giving him a rest and a little grooming?

The T-shirt wasn't much help. It was soon wet and sticky, so I picked up bundles of dry leaves and used those as well. Surprisingly, they weren't bad. Thunder seemed to be enjoying the sensation of being rubbed down and his skin rippled under my hands. The exercise warmed me up, too. I don't suppose it was really cold, after all. It was the middle of summer, but the combination of exhaustion, lateness and tension was making me shiver. I finished off by running my fingers through Thunder's tail and mane and trying to tidy up his forelock, a little like playing with a doll, but he whiffled his nose comfortably against my chest as I did it so it was obviously something he liked.

I took off Thunder's bridle so that he could relax and stretch properly. I had a bottle full of water from the stream so I took a few sips and then poured what was left as best I could into Thunder's mouth, like you would if you were making a pony drink medicine. It wasn't a total success. Quite a lot missed and dribbled down onto my feet, but I did at least feel he wouldn't die of thirst. He snuffled around my feet afterwards, too, licking up the moisture there.

It was just about pitch dark now, except for an occasional gleam from the moon. Clouds must have covered up the sky. There was no point in trying to go anywhere or do anything before it got light. I didn't even know what time it was, since it was much too dark to see my watch. I felt around with my hands until I found the saddle, and curled up so that the middle of my body was underneath it. The stirrups were hard and heavy against me, but the leather gave some warmth and a vague feeling of protection. I bunched up a pile of leaves against my riding hat to create a pillow of sorts, and tried to snuggle down.

All those books that talk about lying on beds of ferns and stuff never mention how hard the ground is, and how cold it is, too. Thankfully, Thunder was standing close to

125

me, so close that I was a little scared that he'd step on me by mistake, despite the saddle. Still, the warmth of his body was too precious to lose. I wished desperately that horses laid down to sleep, so I could have cozied up to his side, but at least he was nearby, making strange snorting noises in his sleep and occasionally moving a few inches one way or the other.

Although I was really tired, I didn't fall asleep for a long time. Oddly enough, the forest was noisier than during the day. There were eerie scufflings and tiny, scary, padding noises, and an owl hooting, and, once, a fierce scream which woke me from a half sleep and made me sit bolt upright, ears straining, heart pounding. Thunder didn't seem at all disturbed, and that comforted me. I lay down again and tried to pretend that I wasn't lost in the middle of a wild forest, but was at home, with Ruby in the bed next to me, and that the heavy breathing I could hear was hers and not Thunder's.

And I tried really, really hard not to think about how she and Dad and everyone must be feeling right now.

I must have dropped off eventually, because suddenly it was getting light, and I was *so* cold, and there were birds singing like crazy. I huddled myself into the tightest possible ball, for warmth, and listened to the dawn chorus. A few birds swooped around from tree to tree and made it feel less lonely, but their singing gradually died away as the light got stronger and the daytime silence of the forest re-established itself. The forest was so protected that there was hardly any dew, which was a shame in terms of drinking, but better for comfort.

My feet were still freezing. I was so stiff, especially my thighs and shoulders, from yesterday's riding, and there were bruises, too, from the falls I'd taken.

I lay with open eyes, studying the sky for a long time as it went from palest gold to blue, and finally a shaft of sunlight penetrated the trees and made a pool of dusty light. Shivering and stiff, I crawled out from under the saddle and went toward the sunlight. It was delicious, like going into a room with a fire blazing in the middle of winter, or jumping into a heated swimming pool. Every part of my body relaxed. Now I realized just how tense I'd been.

I looked around for Thunder. He was standing still under the shade of the trees, his weight on one back foot, asleep. His tail swished as an early morning fly buzzed around his backside, and he lowered his head, as if that had wakened him, and nosed among the leaves for something to eat. I watched as he wandered around the glade, searching and finally finding a patch of scrubby thin grass which he tore up and munched with relish.

"Yes, right, if only I could eat grass, too," I commented, stretching my arms above my head and listening to my stomach rumbling. "Well, boy, what are we going to do today?"

He glanced up at me briefly and pricked up his ears intelligently before dropping his head for a final mouthful.

"We'll need to find a little more grass than that for you, won't we?" I continued. My voice in that silent forest echoed strangely. "And some water might not be a bad idea. What do you think?"

Thunder whickered, that nice soft noise that showed he knew I was talking to him.

"The thing is," I went on slowly, "we're lost. We need to un-lose ourselves, so that Ruby can find us. Does that make sense?"

It seemed to make sense to Thunder. He moved over to

where I was standing in the sun and thrust his nose into my chest the way he liked. I wrapped my arms around his neck.

"Ruby'll want to find us both, because you're hers as well as mine, and because she and I never lose each other. So she'll come. And Dad, probably, and Hannah and Abi. The only question is, where do we go so they can find us?"

I was picking up some welcome heat from Thunder's body and starting to thaw out. The patch of sunlight was moving as the sun rose. It glistened on the bridle, where I'd dumped it last night. I went and got it and rubbed the bit automatically against my sweater to clean it. The two long ends of rein dangled uselessly so I sat down and fiddled them into a knot that would let me ride Thunder properly. Then I went back to him, and slid the reins over his head and put the bit into his mouth, patting him as I did and telling him how sorry I was that he was going to have to keep going for a few more hours, or whatever it took to get somewhere safe. He didn't seem to mind.

I had a close look at the damage to his leg without actually touching it. The ugly flap of skin was still hanging stickily below a raw wound, but there was no bleeding. I was so tempted to try to bind it with my T-shirt, to protect it, but the moment I moved my fingers Thunder pushed his head between my hand and his leg, as if to warn me off.

"If you don't want me to touch it, I won't," I said, soothingly, "but you're being really silly, you know. I could probably make it a lot better."

He snorted as if in answer.

"Okay, let's leave it alone," I sighed. "I just hope it doesn't get gangrene or whatever."

It occurred to me, too, that the value of a pony is affected by a bad scar, but there wasn't much I could do about that, was there? Anyway, Dad was going to be so angry and disappointed with me for running away and getting lost and staying out all night that a drop in Thunder's worth would hardly matter.

I got up and started him walking; at least he wasn't limping. I led him over to the saddle and kept the reins slung over my arm to be safe while I lifted it onto his back. The thought of clambering back into it for yet more riding didn't exactly fill me with joy, but only because I was so tired and worried and stiff. The actual riding didn't bother me one bit any more.

Then, we left our camping place and started off again.

I didn't have the faintest idea which way to go. All day yesterday I'd been able to more or less judge which direction we were going and relate it to an idea of where home was in comparison to the plains. But after the motorcycle incident, I'd lost all sense of where we were, and I had no feeling about which way we'd come through the forest, either. The only thing that seemed like a good idea was going downhill, on the principle that we needed water. That was as good a direction as any, so that's what we did.

I was much more tired than I'd realized at first. It was hard enough to stay upright in the saddle and to ignore my craving for food and drink without worrying about choosing a route. Instead I focused on staying safe and let the reins hang loose. Thunder chose his own path, twisting and turning between the trees. Sometimes he stopped and then I'd pull myself together and kick him on, on the principle that we couldn't just stay in one place. Just as it had yesterday, the forest seemed endless and featureless.

Thunder, however, seemed to know where he was going.

He kept going vaguely downhill, and eventually broke through a tangled thicket of trees and bushes. There, in front of us at long last, was what we'd spent so much time searching for; a stream. He walked straight into the center of it and dropped his head into the cool water, and I was so floppy that I rolled straight off into it, too.

That woke me up, anyway! The water wasn't very deep and luckily the bottom was sandy. I struggled to my feet, dripping, sloshed to the bank, and then squatted down to drink. The water was good, cold and clear, and the headache that had been nagging me since I woke up started to ease miraculously.

Once I'd drunk all I could, I sat back on the bank in a sunny spot and watched Thunder. He was standing, hock-deep in the stream, taking mouthfuls of water and then looking around peacefully.

"Take your time, boy," I said, lazily. "No rush."

Just as I had done yesterday by the gate, I let myself relax so much that I dozed off, curled up in the sun, which shone warmly on me and dried my clothes. I felt much better when I woke up. My headache was gone, and my body seemed to have gotten used to being ravenously hungry. Thunder was grazing quietly on the grass that bordered the stream. He looked up as I sat up, wandered over to me, and nuzzled me affectionately.

"Ready to keep going?" I yawned widely. "Sorry, Thunder, bad manners. Why don't you yawn, anyway?"

I wasn't worried that he'd leave me any longer. I took off the saddle so he could relax and stripped off my damp jeans and sneakers and paddled in the stream, feeling the soft sand between my toes and watching little fish dart away as I got near. If only I could have caught some! I tried using my T-shirt as a net, but it didn't work. I wasn't desperate enough to eat raw fish, and I didn't have any way of making a fire.

I sat on the bank a little longer, drying off again, and then looked to see what time it was. My watch said eight o'clock, which seemed really early, but then I realized the hands weren't moving. It must have stopped when I fell into the stream, and since then I'd been asleep for, how long? Did it actually matter? It was daylight, and that meant we had to find our way home, or at any rate to a place where we could be found, and we had all day to do that.

Just as long as we weren't still lost in the forest when night fell ...

Chapter Twelve

A shiver ran down my back at the thought of another night in the wild. Then I pulled myself together. There had to be search parties out looking for us. I didn't like to think about how Dad and Ruby might be feeling, how they might be imagining me in terrible trouble. But still, starting sometime yesterday, they'd have definitely been out searching. I'd seen television reports on missing children, and the distraught parents, and the lines of policemen and local people beating though the undergrowth. A massive wave of guilt swept through me as I imagined the chaos and fright that I was probably causing.

It was so hard getting started yet again. I felt really mean, making poor Thunder keep going when he must have been totally fed up with this endless journey.

We followed the stream as it wound through the trees. The tinkling, rippling sound it made was nice after the silence we'd been in most of the time. It wasn't fast-flowing, so if Thunder wanted to walk in it, sloshing through and clouding the water with the gravelly sand, rather than next to it, I let him. That way, he chose the easiest path, and I could slump on his back and concentrate on staying put, rather than worrying about routes.

"Because after all, it was you who found the water, not me," I said to him.

It would help clean the cut on his leg, too. Even though Thunder wasn't limping, I had a permanent nagging fear that I'd done something terrible to him. Vague thoughts of infection and gangrene drifted through my mind. Didn't they kill ponies that lost a leg? If that happened, Ruby would never forgive me, and who could blame her?

I was lost in a sort of nightmare scenario, picturing Ruby trying to keep the vet from amputating Thunder's leg, when I felt his pace quicken. The trees were starting to thin out ahead of us. I sat up straight, gripped the reins and pressed my heels against Thunder's sides to show him I was taking control. Carefully, we picked our way over a steep ditch and around some thick brambles at the forest edge, and then, once again, there was the most wonderful moment of emerging from the dark, lifeless forest into the open world.

We were on the plains again and, to my disappointment, there was no road in sight this time. A steep hill soared up ahead, its craggy rocks silhouetted against the blue sky, and trees spread out on either side of me and behind as far as I could see. So, it was a no-brainer deciding which way to go; uphill, away from the woods.

Thunder kept snatching mouthfuls of thin grass, which was fine with me, but I did have to be careful not to tip off forwards every time his head shot down.

"You're getting bad habits, Thunder. Tanya never allows

us to let you eat like this, while we're going along. But I don't blame you, don't worry."

He shook his head, making his mane fly around, and broke into a trot.

"Hey, why all this enthusiasm all of a sudden? Your leg can't be hurting too much, then!"

We were getting near the top of the hill, and I slowed him down as the ground got rougher. Some of the crags were really steep; the sort of thing you'd practice climbing on. For a split second, I remembered the picnic day, and how we'd scrambled around rocks just like these. Just as I was thinking that, there was a shout.

"Poppy! Poppy! Poppy! It's me!"

I pulled Thunder in and stood up in the stirrups, looking around wildly. Where? Who?

"Over here!"

There was a clatter of hoofs and suddenly there was my twin, throwing herself off a pony and grabbing at me, dragging me off Thunder and then hugging and hugging me as if she'd never stop.

"Ruby?"

I couldn't believe what was happening. The contrast between being all alone with Thunder for so long and this was too much. Part of me wondered if I was hallucinating, the way they do in the desert. Maybe thirst and hunger were driving me crazy?

But Ruby's voice didn't fade away.

"Poppy, are you okay? Where have you been? What happened? We've been so scared ..."

"Ruby?" I said again, slowly.

"Yes, it's me. Wake up, Poppy, it's all right, you're safe now."

134

I was vaguely aware of more people and ponies, of familiar voices.

"Is she all right?"

"I think so, but it's weird. She's not talking properly."

"She isn't hurt, is she?"

"Not that I can see. Poppy, say something!"

My sister's insistent voice broke through my uncertainty. I just stood there and let her hug me.

"Ruby, I'm really, really sorry ..."

"It doesn't matter, no one's going to be angry. We just want you to be safe."

"Poppy, we're so glad to have you back, aren't we, Abi?"

I recognized Hannah's voice, but I was still struggling to confess.

"Ruby, it's about Thunder, I've made him hurt his leg."

Now she'd lose patience with me, and hate me for ruining her pony.

"Who's more important, you or the pony? Don't be silly, Poppy. Use some sense!"

There was something incredibly comforting about the way she was telling me off, as usual, and, strangely, she didn't seem to be angry about Thunder. In fact, she didn't seem very interested in him. I felt so confused.

She led me over to a low rock and made me sit down, still with her arms around me. I looked around and saw Hannah holding Thunder and Socks. The two ponies were nuzzling each other. Then Abi, with Henry and Smoke trailing behind her, knelt down next to me and held out a sandwich.

"Come on, have something to eat, you must be starving," she said. Her cheerful, matter of fact tone helped.

I pulled myself together and sat up properly. Things sort of came into focus and I was able to smile with relief at my three closest friends.

"Wow, yes, I am," I said gratefully, grabbing the sandwich and taking the most enormous mouthful.

"There's water, too. Are you thirsty?"

I shook my head. "Not very, we found a stream today. Yesterday, we were desperate for water."

"You've had a real adventure," said Ruby, envy in her voice. "I'm so proud of you!"

I nearly choked. "Proud? For getting lost and damaging your pony?"

"What *is* all this about hurting Thunder, anyway? What've you done to him?"

My heart sank completely as Ruby went over to look. Now for the worst ...

"He got a graze," Hannah said, peering. "Look, on his leg there."

"It's not too bad," Abi commented.

Ruby hadn't said a word yet. She was touching Thunder's leg very carefully and feeling the wound.

"If it's infected, it'll smell bad," Hannah said. She leaned forward and sniffed cautiously.

We all gazed at Thunder in awful fascination.

After a long pause, Ruby said, "It doesn't look bad to me, and there's no sign of any infection. Why should there be? It's only a cut."

"And you looked after him," Abi added, comfortingly.

"He wouldn't let me touch it," I admitted, ashamed. "I just left it overnight, but today we rode through a stream, and that cleaned it a little."

"So, stop panicking," Ruby said. "It's not a big deal,

Poppy. You know what, you've got to learn to take things less seriously." She came over and hugged me again to show she wasn't being horrible.

"There'll be a scar," I said, fearfully.

"So what? He's okay. You just rode him here and he wasn't limping, was he?"

"No, but his value ..." I gulped. "What'll Dad say? He'll kill me!"

"Don't be silly, he'll be so relieved to know that you're safe that he won't say a word, you'll see. Thunder's fine. You looked after him well. Dad'll understand."

"That reminds me. Do we have cell phone reception here?" shrieked Hannah. "We've got to tell him that we've found them."

Abi took out her phone and looked at the face.

"No, but we did down by the parking lot, I'll just get over there and report in. Brace yourself, Poppy, there'll be hordes of people here as soon as they know we've found you."

Abi jumped onto Henry and cantered off downhill.

"I don't understand, what parking lot?"

"You know, where we had that picnic? Don't you remember it?"

"Of course I do. Actually, that's where I was aiming for in the first place, yesterday, but we got kind of lost."

"Well, you got there in the end, just a little late."

"Better late than never, eh?" said Hannah. "Hey, Poppy, I can't wait to hear all about it. I'd never have dared to do what you did, going off on your own like that."

"And tricking everyone for a long time. What time did you actually set off?"

I thought back. "Around six, but then I had to go home

137

and get clothes and food and stuff, and then get Thunder and everything. Tanya saw me, didn't she?"

"Yes, but she thought you were me, so no one raised the alarm. We didn't wake up till noon, and then we just thought you'd gone home. Later on, of course, Tanya realized 'I' hadn't come back, and then all hell broke loose."

"Gosh, so how long have you been searching for me?"

"Yesterday afternoon, and then overnight there wasn't much anyone could do, and then this morning we asked if we could try together. I just had a feeling that you might be coming here."

"Your dad tried here yesterday, and of course you were nowhere to be seen," added Hannah.

"Is he okay?" I asked anxiously.

"He will be now." Hannah smiled comfortingly.

"I didn't see anyone the whole time except some bikers, and they didn't see me." I explained what had happened.

"They did. They reported that they'd seen you, but not until this morning when they heard about you on the news. They were so upset that they'd frightened you off. They didn't mean to."

"I know, it's just that the motorcycles were so loud, poor Thunder had the scare of his life."

"Exactly, but they said he'd bolted with you into the woods. That's where Dad and most of the searchers are, combing through the forest, but it's massive."

"Don't I know it! We were lost in it for hours and hours and hours."

"What did you do when it got dark?" Ruby sounded awed.

I shrugged. "We went to sleep. There wasn't much else we could do."

"Weren't you scared? I'd have been petrified."

"It was all right," I reassured my twin. "Not really spooky at all. Thunder was with me, don't forget."

She opened her mouth to say something but there was a breathless shout from Abi, who was urging Henry up the hill toward us.

"I got through; they know, and your dad actually started crying!" she yelled.

Ruby and I looked at each other. "Wow," we both said, awed.

Abi slid off Henry and plunked herself down next to us.

"Can I have that last sandwich if you don't want it?" she said.

That made us laugh, and then Abi saw the funny side of it and started laughing too. Soon the four of us were rolling around on the grass, giggling hysterically.

We waited where we were for the search party to join us. All four ponies had their heads down, grazing happily. The noontime sun was hot, my stomach was full of solid food, and I was surrounded by my best friends. I just hoped Dad wasn't too upset with me.

Hannah was looking back to the forest and was the first to see them all emerging – a huge crowd of police and civilians, and at the front, there was Dad. He yelled something as he saw us, and started to sprint up the hill toward us. Instinctively, I ran too, so that we met about halfway. He grabbed me in his arms and held me so close I couldn't breathe, and then swung me around and around, so that my legs were flying through the air, all the time going, "Poppy, Poppy, my little Poppy!"

He sort of collapsed onto the grass and I tumbled next to him, and Ruby ran to be under his spare arm. The three of us lay in a heap, closer together than we'd been for years.

"Poppy my pet, whatever would your mother have said if I'd lost you?" Dad said finally.

I'd never thought about that. Mom died a long time ago and we didn't really remember her or even talk about her much. But Dad obviously did think about her, and felt an obligation to her to look after us properly. How terrible it must have been for him, not only to know that I'd gone missing, but also to feel it was all his responsibility.

I knew I was going to have to be brave and tell the truth about what had happened, but now that Dad had shown his vulnerable side it was somehow easier.

"I'm really sorry. I didn't mean to get lost and get everyone so scared," I started. "I just wanted to prove I could ride Thunder."

"And she did," Ruby put in, loyally, squeezing my arm.

"I had no idea you felt so badly about him," Dad said, not seeming to listen to what I was saying. "If only I'd gotten rid of him right away, when Tanya told me he was too big for you."

"She didn't, Dad. She just said I'd need to grow into him a little."

"Well, you won't have to, not now. My mind's made up. I'm not going to have anyone say that I bully my own children into something they can't handle."

"But Dad ..." Ruby and I spoke together, united in horror, but Dad wasn't paying attention.

"That pony's going, the moment we can get rid of him. Today, preferably, but if not, tomorrow. That's it, Poppy, I won't have you terrorized by any horse. You'll never have to see him again."

Chapter Thirteen

There was a stunned silence.

"But Dad!" I started, at the same moment that Ruby gasped, "You can't!"

We both talked over each other but Dad wasn't listening. He'd turned away to talk to a policeman, and when I grabbed his arm he just patted it comfortingly, but he wasn't listening! In fact, he actually went, "Shush now, girls. Give me a moment."

We gazed at each other in open-mouthed horror. So that was it. I'd messed up big time now. My attempt to prove myself had completely backfired.

There was no chance to try to change Dad's mind. We were surrounded by all the people who'd turned out to find me, and I had to answer questions and reassure Tanya and Hannah's mother and the police that I was absolutely fine, that no one had attacked me, or made me want to run away in the first place. There was even a television reporter who insisted on asking lots of pointless questions while a cameraman recorded everything.

Tanya took charge of Thunder. Between the bodies all around me, I caught a glimpse of her checking him over and then she mounted him carefully and started off down the hill. I shouted, but she didn't hear over the noise of everyone talking at once. Ruby saw, too, and squirmed through the crowd and ran after her, but it was too late. They were cantering steadily away from us. Could this be the very last time we saw our pony?

Once it was established that I wasn't injured or anything, we were finally allowed to start for home. Ruby, Hannah and Abi got back on their ponies. Ruby was fighting back tears and trying to hide them from everyone.

Abi and Hannah waved encouragingly as they trotted off. I watched as they got smaller and smaller, and wished desperately that I was with them.

They went downhill so they could join the road and then ride alongside it until they reached the main road back to the village. They'd been told to stick to the road, rather than cut across the plains, just in case they got lost, too. I could see us being told that a lot from now on.

A lot of the searchers dispersed, too, walking back through the forest or going to the road and waiting to be picked up there by friends. Dad and I were left with a policewoman, who was very kind, but neither of them let me speak. Every time I tried they shushed me and told me to rest.

Eventually the policewoman's radio beeped and she led us down to the road where a police car was waiting. We got in the back. Dad was holding my hand really tightly, as if he was frightened he'd lose me again. We had to go to the police station to make a statement, so it was hours and hours before we got home. Ruby was over at Hannah's and her mother insisted on escorting her back to our place, even though we'd been allowed to go between houses alone during the summer. It looked like my escapade was going to have long reaching and rather unpleasant consequences, even forgetting what might happen to Thunder.

By the time we were finally alone, just the three of us, I felt as if I'd been bottling up my emotions so much that I'd burst. I could tell Ruby was just the same. Dad disappeared into his study and made a long phone call, and we tried to listen in, but he kept his voice down.

"I'm sure it's about Thunder," I whispered.

"Yes. Do you think he's sending him away?"

I shrugged in despair. "He's made his mind up, and I don't see what we can do. You know what he's like. He'll do anything for us, preferably involving some sort of action. The trouble is, he doesn't necessarily stop to find out what we want.'

Ruby held my hand comfortingly. "That's really wise, Poppy. He means *so* well."

"It's all my fault, isn't it? If I hadn't been such a wimp all summer, if I hadn't been so stupid as to go and get lost ..."

"Well, it wasn't *all* your fault. I was mean to you, too. I've been bullying you, haven't I? I don't know, I seemed to forget what you're really like and to expect you to be a completely different person."

"I don't much like what I've been like," I said fiercely. "I want to be like you."

"But you're Poppy and I'm Ruby – and we're twins and best friends, but we're not clones, remember?"

143

She looked into my eyes with absolute conviction and I found myself nodding in agreement.

"Friends again?"

"Friends again, always," I answered.

"Listen!" she hissed.

Dad had raised his voice slightly and we heard him say, "Seven thirty."

A few seconds later, he came out of the study, practically falling over us.

"Twins, what on earth are you doing there? Not listening, I hope?"

"You can't blame us. It's our pony you want to get rid of," said Ruby, her voice angry.

Dad took her by the arm and spoke to her gently, but as if I wasn't there.

"Ruby, just think, for one moment, about what's happened. When Tanya told me how much Poppy's been avoiding riding Thunder, how scared she's been ... How can you possibly suggest that we keep him? How selfish would that be?"

"But ..."

"Ruby, you've got to think about your sister and not yourself. She's tried her best, I'm sure, but her best wasn't enough, and now the clear way out of the situation is to forget all about Thunder. I know Poppy; she'll try to pretend she doesn't want him to go to please you, but this time we need to think about what she really feels."

"Dad, you've got to listen," I said urgently. "You've got it all wrong. I don't want to lose Thunder, not now. Please, you have to change your mind!"

He cuddled me up close to him and kissed my forehead. "Sweetheart, you're in shock," he said, soothingly. "It's really late, and you need some sleep."

"No, not yet. This is the most important thing I've ever had to say to you," I insisted. "I can't bear it if you get rid of Thunder. I'll never be happy ever again. You have to change your mind. You have to!"

"Yes, yes, yes, Poppy," he murmured. "Never mind about all that now. We'll talk in the morning, when you've calmed down."

"But that'll be too late!" Ruby wailed. She was crying now, tears running down her face.

"Ruby, I've said this before; no more, all right?"

I opened my mouth to speak again but he went on without taking a breath. "Now, both of you, no more drama. It's been such a long day, neither of you can possibly be thinking straight. I want you to both go up to your own bedrooms. I'll bring you each some supper in bed, and then, after a good night's sleep, we can all start afresh."

He just didn't let us get a word in edgeways. It would almost have been funny that he was feeling so guilty about bullying me into riding Thunder that now he was bullying me into losing him, if it hadn't been such a disastrous situation. We had to get into bed, and he told us we weren't to talk, and even after we'd eaten our separate suppers he kept popping upstairs to see how we were. We didn't even get a chance to sneak into each other's rooms until it was really late, after he'd finally gone to bed himself.

I tiptoed out of my room and bumped into Ruby doing exactly the same thing. We suppressed instant nervous giggles and automatically went into her room, the one that used to be ours, and huddled under the comforter together so that we could talk without running the risk of being overheard.

"What're we going to do?" I whispered urgently.

"First things first; is Dad right? You don't want to sell Thunder, do you? Because if that's so ..."

"No!"

"Shhh," she hissed, "he'll hear us! Okay, but you did, didn't you?"

"He's right about that. I almost hated Thunder most of the summer, but that wasn't really his fault. It was mine. I was so petrified about riding him, it became a sort of obsession. That's why, in the end, the only thing I could think to do was to go off on my own and show myself I could manage. And I did."

"I know, I could tell right away when we saw you. You can ride really well all of a sudden; it's strange."

"Just confidence, I suppose. There were a few sticky moments, I have to admit. I'll tell you about them later. What do we do now?"

"Well, what do *you* want?" She sounded just like Dad.

"Right now there's nothing I want more than to keep Thunder and ride him all I can – as long as we share him properly."

"Okay, so we both think the same. How do we change Dad's mind?"

"If it's not too late already. I'm sure that phone call was about sending him away tomorrow first thing."

"I bet you're right. But it's not too late. We just have to stop it from happening."

I found myself giggling again. "We could run away with Thunder!"

Ruby was laughing too. "Don't let Dad hear us! Oh yes, I can just see that policewoman's face if she has to start searching again, only for two of us this time."

"The awful thing is, that might make them think Dad was horrible to us, or something."

That thought sobered us up instantly.

"And he's only trying to do what he thinks is best. No more running away. But what else?" I felt totally despairing.

"Just talking to him. We don't have a hope." She ran a finger over a stray tear that was running down her cheek, and gulped.

Somehow, Ruby being the weak one made me stronger. "Who's being negative now? He's not an ogre, he's our Dad, and he's just gotten himself into a muddle, trying to protect us. Let's confront him and make him realize he's got it all wrong."

"You *have* changed," Ruby said, looking at me with new respect. "All right. He'll be up early, I bet, to sort everything out, so we have to be awake by dawn."

"We need to talk to the others," I said. "They'll help. I'm so tired, I can't think straight anymore."

"Hannah's got a cell phone, I'll try her first, and maybe she'll have been talking to Abi."

"She's sure to have been. What happened while you were at Hannah's?"

Ruby shrugged. "We weren't alone much. Everyone kept fussing over us, and Abi had to go home right away. We weren't sure what you really felt, any more than Dad does."

"Well, you know now. Let's sneak downstairs and call Hannah."

Even though the situation was so drastic, it was still thrilling, sneaking down to the kitchen and whispering into the phone so that Dad couldn't possibly hear. Hannah answered at once, and she was already on her house phone with Abi, so we could just all hear each other.

"So what do we do?" Ruby asked, despairingly. "If we're not quick, we'll lose Thunder. I'm sure Dad's arranged for him to be taken away first thing, and you know how impossible it is to make him change his mind when he thinks he's doing what's best for us."

"I have an idea," whispered Abi. "You might think it's a little stupid, but it's the best I can come up with."

She explained her plan, with translation from Hannah whenever we couldn't hear her well.

"That's great," I hissed. "Let's go for it."

"Sure?"

"Yes, Dad won't be able to ignore us. Abi, you're an angel!"

"Six o'clock at the stables, then?" Hannah checked.

"Don't oversleep! We'll be there."

We placed the phone back onto its base and froze when it made that little ping noise, but Dad must have been fast asleep. Then we tiptoed back to our old room.

"Can you stay awake?" Ruby whispered.

I yawned. "I wish I could say yes, but honestly, I had so little sleep last night and the night before that my eyes want to close by themselves."

"Don't worry, I'm not that tired. It's my turn tonight. Go to sleep and don't worry about a thing."

I didn't intend to, but I fell asleep almost instantly and it only felt like a second before Ruby was shaking and shushing me at the same time. I was still in her bed, and she was crouching next to it.

"Wake up! It's six fifteen – we'll be late!"

"Any sound from Dad?"

"Not yet. Hurry!"

We dressed quickly and slipped downstairs. I squeezed the front door open and shut it quietly behind us. Then we sprinted through the silent village to the stables.

Hannah and Abi were waiting for us, bursting with suppressed excitement, hiding under the shelter of the stable roof.

"He's back in the stall," Abi told us. "Hannah's got the rope, look."

Hannah was weighed down with an assortment of ropes and reins. She shared them between us and we looked at each other.

"Okay, girls, this is it," Ruby said seriously.

We nodded solemnly and let ourselves into Thunder's stall. He was watching us curiously. I patted his neck.

"Darling Thunder, I know you're going to think we're crazy, but this is for your own good, it really is," I murmured.

He thrust his nose against me and whickered contentedly.

"Nice one, Thunder," said Ruby. "Don't forget you're mine too now, will you?"

I glanced to check that she wasn't mad, but she was smiling even though her face was pale with tension. It was all right, then.

"Do we have to start now?" asked Abi, struggling to unravel the long leading rein she'd been given. "He's not exactly going to like it, is he?"

"Let's wait till we hear them coming," suggested Hannah.

I looked at my watch. "They won't be long, not if we were right about 7:30."

"We'll look pretty stupid if we're wrong," Abi grinned nervously.

149

"Come on, let's go!"

We knotted ropes or reins around our waists, like mountaineers. It felt deadly serious, and yet we were all stifling giggles and didn't dare meet each other's eyes.

And then we tied ourselves closely to Thunder. I attached myself to his noseband, Ruby wound her rope around his neck, Hannah tied herself to his off foreleg, and Abi clipped the rein onto the head collar more effectively than I'd managed two days ago. We ducked and wound around each other, too, to create a complex, unbreakable web of rope.

Thunder was amazing. He must have thought we were crazy, but he still stood patiently. He breathed heavily down Abi's neck, tickling her, and I fed him handfuls of hay from his net with my free hand to keep him calm.

Then we waited.

The early morning silence was broken by the rumbling of vehicles. We couldn't see, but we could hear Dad greeting someone. He sounded stressed and worried, not at all like his usual confident self. Then we heard Tanya's higher voice, and the voices came nearer. We tensed ourselves, I wrapped the slack of my rope tighter around my wrist, and then they saw us.

For a split second all three adults, Dad, Tanya and a strange man, stood open-mouthed, staring at us. I suppose it must have been quite a sight – one pony and four girls, inextricably linked together.

Then a wide grin spread over Tanya's face, and at the same moment Dad burst into gales of laughter.

"Girls, girls, what are you doing here?" he spluttered. "You're supposed to be in bed, safe and sound."

"They've made their minds up, you know," said Tanya. "They don't want to lose their pony, do you, girls?"

Dad sobered up. "Girls, this really isn't the best time," he said.

"No, Dad," said Ruby, sternly. "It's got to be now. You've made a terrible mistake, and we have to explain."

"You're too right. I did make a mistake, buying you that pony, but you don't have to worry. He's going to the sales yard. He'll be gone, and you'll never have to think about him again."

"We don't want anything but Thunder, Dad," I said, firmly.

He looked at me, his mouth open.

"I've been trying to tell you ever since yesterday," I carried on. "I don't want to lose him any more than Ruby does."

He looked as if he was struggling to understand.

"Look, girls, I appreciate how much you both like ponies. Before all this started, you were so happy coming here and riding Smoke and whatshisname ..."

"Dandy."

"Yes, Dandy. And then I messed up, I realize that now, by trying to be clever and all that."

"But I loved Thunder right from the start!"

I made a face at Ruby – she'd really said the wrong thing this time.

"Exactly my point. You were happy but Poppy wasn't, and that's because she's a much less confident rider. Tanya explained it all to me. I just wish I'd realized before."

Ruby tried to speak but I got in first.

"You're so right, Dad. I couldn't cope with Thunder and I've been very unhappy this summer."

"There you are!"

"But that's all changed. Why do you think I went off on my own like I did?"

151

"Because we've all been making you miserable, so miserable that you had to run away. That's why I feel so awful. I've failed you, Poppy."

"No, you haven't!" I insisted. "I didn't need to take Thunder, did I? If I'd hated him that much, why would I take him? I could have run off on foot, easily."

"Or taken Dandy," added Ruby, helpfully.

"Yes, or taken Dandy. But I didn't. I took Thunder, because I knew I had to sort this out by myself. Not because the others thought I was a coward, which they did, and not because you wouldn't listen to me when I tried to talk to you …"

I paused. Dad had gone very white and was looking at me as if he'd never really heard me speak before.

"I went because I needed to prove to myself that I could manage him, and not only that, enjoy him. And I succeeded, Dad. I made it. Okay, we got lost and I caused all sorts of mayhem and I'm really and truly sorry to have scared you and stuff, but none of that was planned. I should have gotten back safely that afternoon, before anyone panicked. And what I wanted to find out was what I did find out. I love Thunder, too, and I can ride him and I want to keep on sharing him with Ruby forever."

I don't think I'd ever spoken to Dad for so long at one time. There was a long silence.

Then he smiled the widest, warmest smile.

"My brave girl. Just like your mother."

"So, can we keep Thunder?" I kept my head high but my voice wobbled a little.

"Well," he said slowly, "there is still the problem that I never thought about, of only one of you being able to ride at a time."

152

"We don't care, Dad. We can share, really we can!"

He went on as if we hadn't spoken. "So maybe we can arrange to use one of the stable ponies as well ..."

I held my breath. I could feel Ruby trembling beside me. Surely that meant ...

"Yes, that's the way. He's yours, girls. Thunder's your very own pony, as I said on your birthday, and he's still yours. For good."

The loudest ever whoop of joy erupted from the four of us. Thunder tossed his head and stepped back in alarm, pulling us off our feet, but none of us cared. Somehow, we scrambled back up and crazily hugged each other and Thunder.

From now on, we'd all be staying together.